AMBER ARGYLE

OF
SAND
AND
STORM

FAIRY QUEENS 5

First Edition: August 2016
Library of Congress Cataloging-in-Publication Data
LCCN: 2016914564

Argyle, Amber
Of Sand and Storm (Fairy Queens Series) – 1st ed
ISBN-13: 978-0-9976390-2-5

Visit Amber Argyle's website to sign up for her free starter library or to learn more: amberargyle.com

To all those who have lost
the choice over what happens to their bodies,
past and present.

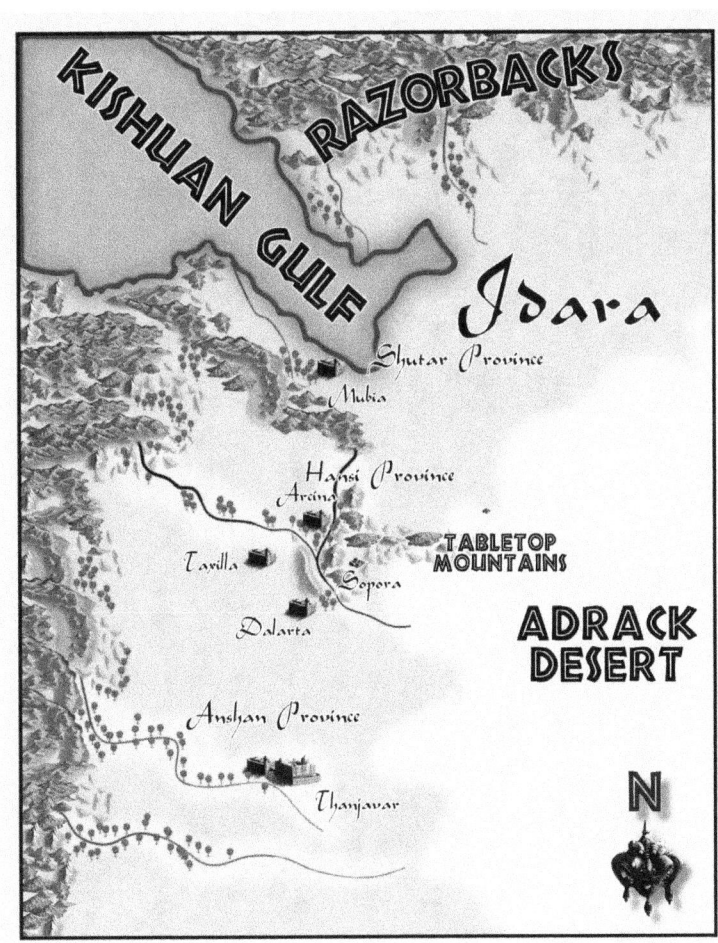

CHAPTER ONE

In the predawn haze, Cinder held her cloak tight to ward off the chill as she hurried down the nearly empty street. Before her, a ragged man whistling an eerie tune pushed a cart filled with piss pots he had collected during the night. Cinder found herself counting the beats of the song, a child's rhyme she couldn't place. She held her veil tight over her mouth and breathed shallowly, trying not to notice the liquid sloshing in the pots.

Glad she hadn't eaten breakfast, she arrived at the tannery twelve steps ahead of the man. But when she opened the door and stepped into the crumbling building, the fetid stench sent her straight back outside. The man with the piss pots chuckled under his breath just before Cinder lifted her veil and vomited bile onto the ground in the alley. A pile of dirty blankets shifted and a drunk squinted at her. He cursed her roundly before turning over, his fleas jumping grumpily at the interruption.

She wiped her mouth with the back of her arm, then blotted her face to make sure she hadn't sweated off her dark makeup. So far so good. Counting to ten to calm down, Cinder forced herself to march back to the tannery—past the piss-pot man, who watched her with close-set black eyes above an equally black veil. She entered the dimly lit building with its long row of hides stretched tightly across frames. Men stood scraping off the fur with flint or steel or stone. The early morning breeze flowed through an open door to the back yard, where men and women stirred the huge pots of leather soaking in urine or dye.

Cinder made sure her veil was in place and looked around nervously. The man who'd been pushing the cart leaned against a wall, one skinny leg cocked as he looked at her. Something about him seemed off, like he didn't belong here. Her gaze lingered on his clothes, and she realized it was because he was so clean.

Before she could dwell on it, a man in black robes approached her. His hands were stained unnaturally dark. "What you want?" he growled.

Three little words, but the answer to his question would take dozens. "A job," Cinder said simply, keeping her eyes downcast so he couldn't see the silver of them.

She felt him studying her, no doubt noticing her worn but clean and serviceable robes. "Are you pregnant?" he asked.

She nearly forgot to keep her eyes down. "No, sir."

"Runaway?"

Pursing her lips in anger, Cinder shook her head.

"Listen, girl, this is no place for someone with other options. Go back to your parents. Or your lover. Or wherever else you came from. Only the truly desperate come here. And you aren't there yet." The man turned his back and started away.

Cinder stared at his retreating figure. Fifteen weeks of searching, one hundred and five days of sneering and spitting and curses. She hurried after him and grasped his arm. "Please." The word nearly burned her tongue. "I've already been everywhere else."

Her eyes remained downcast, but she could feel him staring at her. Two fingers suddenly brushed down her nose. She jerked back, but not before he had a smudge of her dark makeup on his fingertips. Stepping forward, he grabbed her chin and yanked off her veil. "Are you an escaped slave?" His dark eyes bore into her traitorous silver ones. "Because if you are, I'll call the city guard right now. I don't need the fines and—"

"No!" Cinder jerked back from his bruising grip, but not before he'd ripped her headscarf off, tearing out a tendril of her hair with it. Her gold locks tumbled down her shoulders like a confession.

He threw the headscarf at her. "Slave," he hissed.

Six other men stopped their scraping and looked up at Cinder. The piss-pot man simply watched, the crinkle around one eye suggesting that under his veil he wore a crooked grin. Cinder clenched her sweaty fists, eight fingernails digging into two palms. "I am not a slave!" As proof, she pointed to the freeborn tattoo above her ear, on the strip of scalp she fastidiously shaved clean every night.

The man stared at it in the dim light, his mouth turning to a sneer of disgust. "Then you have no master to reimburse when you are dead."

Cinder slid her hand into her robe and gripped the kitchen knife she'd pilfered earlier, though she did not draw it. "I was born an Idaran." She choked on the words—she hated Idara and its people as much as they hated her. It goaded her to claim them as her own. But goaded was better than dead.

"You'll never be an Idaran," barked the man just before he spat in her face. His saliva ran wet and lumpy down her cheek. Starting to count down silently, Cinder wiped off the spit with her sleeve and backed toward the door.

Five . . .

"A clanman killed my sons," a voice said from right behind her. She whipped around to find an old man, bits of fur clinging to him like a dirty aura, between her and the door. He held a sharpened chunk of flint in his calloused hands.

Four . . .

Cinder slid the knife free. "Harm me, and the city guard will see you all beheaded. I am an Idaran citizen. I have rights."

Three . . .

A woman darkened the door, gripping a thick, stained stick. "Only because the false lord is a clannish sympathizer," she lisped through her missing teeth.

Two . . .

"Their filthy goddess murdered my wife," an older man said as he circled closer.

Cinder had been all over Arcina, searching for a job. She had faced hostility, but never like this. Several more filthy-handed men crowded toward her. One of them licked his lips hungrily, untied a matted belt from his waist, and wound it around his hands. All the while the piss-pot man watched, amusement flashing across his deep-set eyes.

One . . .

Rage and fear lanced through Cinder's belly. By the Balance, she was sick of the hatred of those who didn't even know her. She slashed her knife through the air to drive back her would-be attackers. Next, she slipped under the grasping hands of the old man and danced out of the arms of a woman.

Zero . . .

Cinder bolted through the door, burst into the gray morning light that matched her traitor eyes and sprinted down the street, her blond hair streaming behind her. She counted each of her steps, pushing the numbers to come faster, faster. The men and woman from the tannery gave chase, their voices angry and hateful. Above it all, she could hear the laughter of the piss-pot man. But unlike her pursuers, Cinder was young and strong. She turned corners and whipped past a few early stragglers. If it had been any other time of day, her pursuers likely would have incited a mob. This early in the morning, even the criminals were drunk or abed.

When her lungs threatened to burst and her legs trembled, Cinder dove into an alley and huddled behind some empty crates, her heartbeat pounding in her temples. She listened for the sound of pursuit—threats and pounding footfalls—but could only hear a distant birdsong and the frantic beating of her heart. Panic welled up so strong that she thought it might choke her. She pinched her eyes shut and started counting. One ragged breath, two clenched fists, three racing heartbeats. She concentrated, counting out the time between exhalations and inhalations.

Still, it was a long time before she dared to peek out into the street, and only fear made her do it. If she wasn't at the House of Night in time to bring Zura her breakfast, Cinder's debt would only increase. After shaking out her cramped limbs, she rewrapped her headscarf over her hair four times, tied up her veil, and hustled down two streets before she finally had her bearings. She was in the warehouse district—over a league from the House of Night. Matching her step to the cadence of eight beats, she ran through the streets, which were already filling with people. She avoided the market—she couldn't risk being seen—instead sticking to the familiar cloth-maker's district.

When Cinder finally reached the rear of the compound, the oppressive heat had arrived and drenched her with sweat. She slipped through the gate and paused to insert her tension wrench and pick to turn the lock back into place. Lips moving soundlessly, she counted each of her tools before shoving them into the compartment she'd sewn into the wrap around her breasts. Then she raced across the exquisite gardens, her feet flying over twenty-nine flagstones, and burst into the servant house.

Inside the massive kitchen her grandmother, Storm, was already pacing, wringing her hands with anxiety. Her head snapped up when Cinder entered. Their matching silver gazes locked. "Did they hire you?"

Cinder gave a one-two shake of her head.

Her grandmother's face tightened. "The younger girls have already served the companions and patrons." She pushed the tray with Zura's breakfast into Cinder's hands. "Run, girl. Else we'll both be caned."

Cinder rushed from the kitchen, through the colonnade, and into the mansion, the porcelain dishes on the tray rattling dangerously. Zura's gentlemen thugs—brothers by the name of Farush and Farood—stood side by side at the doorway that lead to Zura's office. Their scalps always gleamed with oil to show off their tattoos, and their beards were always perfectly curled. From experience, Cinder knew they put the same care and precision into their canings.

She felt the thugs' amused gazes on her as she paused and used her sleeve to mop up three drops of spilled tea. She forced her breathing to slow and pushed open the door. Inside the office, Zura's daughter, Magian, stood on a wooden box, her delicate head bent over a ledger on the long table before her. Behind the small woman was a door that led to Zura's personal rooms. That door was flanked by twenty-eight cubes filled with an uneven assortment of ledgers and scrolls that always made Cinder's fingers twitch to even them out. The wall to her left was taken up by heavy wooden cabinets, where Zura kept the companions' fine jewelry. The sparkles and colors would never know true sunlight, only the half-light of the oil lamps.

With her gray hair swept back in an elegant bun, Zura stood before the pivot glass doors, clasping her hands behind her back. She stared out at the front courtyard with its whimpering fountains—the dry season was almost at an end—and limp palm trees. The gardens featured a section dedicated to each of the four nations, just as the House of Night sold women from every country.

Cinder rested the tray on the table and settled Magian's breakfast next to the ledger. Next, Cinder placed Zura's flatbread, covered in goat cheese and fruit preserves, on the low table in front of the rich velvet cushions, and poured sweet tea into the cup. Cinder's mouth watered—she'd been up six hours and had yet to eat anything. She rose smoothly to her feet and stepped back. "Will that be all, Mother?"

Zura turned away from the light, her face cast in shadow. Streaks of near white spread from her temples like a badger's mask. She was a handsome woman, or would have been if she ever deigned to offer something so common as a smile. "Why are you late?" Her voice was low and precise.

Cinder inhaled. *One, two, three.* Exhaled. *One, two, three.* "I overslept. It won't happen again."

"Do not lie to me."

Sweat dotted Cinder's brow, and she remembered her dark makeup. She considered lying, or only giving part of the truth. But she had no way of knowing how much Zura had pieced together. "I am not one of your companions, Zura. I am a freewoman."

Zura stepped forward to slowly circle Cinder. "You are my servant, bound to obey my orders. I have forbidden anyone from leaving the compound at night—it's too dangerous with the gangs of thieves that the false lord seems incapable of stopping." She paused and said over Cinder's shoulder, "And you will address me as 'Mother.'"

Cinder ground her teeth—calling Zura "Mother" was a mockery. And Cinder was always too busy with chores during the day to step foot outside the compound. The only time left to her was the early mornings. She barely slept anymore, but sleep was a price she'd been willing to pay for a chance at freedom.

Zura flared out her robes, revealing her bilious trousers, and sat on the velvet cushions. Her clothing was made of exceeding-

7

ly fine linen, expertly pleated. She rolled the flatbread around the cheese and preserves and took a dainty bite. "Now, tell me why you were sneaking out."

Cinder clenched all twenty-eight of her teeth and said nothing.

Zura took a sip of her tea before carefully setting the cup back onto the tray. "Magian," she said with false gentleness, "look up Cinder in the ledger."

Without a word, Magian moved off her box, carried it to the shelves, and stepped up to grasp one of the many ledgers. She lugged the ponderous thing to the side of the table nearest Cinder and set it down. Standing on her box, Magian flipped through the pages of accounts of slaves and servants until she reached Cinder's family.

Now she turned the pages more slowly. Cinder recognized her grandmother's name, Storm, written across the top. Cinder knew the ledger had detailed notes about her grandmother's purchase price, thirty-three silvers, as well as her patrons—how much they had paid as well as notes about their social status. The next section was Cinder's mother's. Although Ash had only been an infant when she'd arrived on a slaving ship, it had been enough to mark her as a slave. Her purchase price was much less than Storm's, but her client list was even longer. The third section was for Holla—her purchase price was only a handful of bavas, copper coins worth little. She had been slow in speech and thought, but she'd proven to be a determined worker. It was Holla who had minded Cinder during her baby and toddler years, while her mother and grandmother were busy with their patrons. It was Holla who had kept her out of trouble.

The next section was dedicated to Cinder. Seventeen years' worth of numbers dancing across the page. It seemed her whole life was made up of numbers. Every meal, every scrap of clothing, every *inconvenience* carefully noted. One hundred and twenty attalics—small silver coins. And every day she lived and ate at the House of Night was another coin subtracted from her wages. In short, it would take her over two decades—7,359 days, to be precise—to pay off her debt. And that was if she managed to avoid any extra expenses, like a healer.

"Now," Zura said, "tell me again why you are at liberty to do whatever you wish."

Because I am free. Or should be. But Cinder remained silent, refusing to give voice to the words burning her up from the inside out.

Zura sighed and pulled a small vellum scroll from her breast pocket. She held it out to Cinder. "Read it." When Cinder didn't take it, the older woman chuckled. "Ah, I remember. You can't read." Humiliation flared hot across Cinder's face. She had worked hard to recognize some names and knew her numbers, but she was far from literate. Zura gestured to Magian, who took the scroll from her mistress's hand.

Zura sat back on her cushions, satisfied as a cat as Magian read, "'The girl has stopped at nearly every district in the city, looking for work. All of them have turned her away.'"

Cinder forced her face to reveal nothing. Zura'd had her followed. Cinder tried to remember if there had been anyone familiar. The only person that came to mind was the piss-pot man with his too-clean clothes. But she would probably never be certain. How long had Zura known?

"Is my employment not sufficient for you?" the older woman said. "That you would rather work in a filthy tannery?"

Cinder wanted to scream that she hadn't done anything wrong—she'd merely been looking for work. "Mother, if I am ever to pay my debt to you, I must find work elsewhere."

"They would pay you less than I!" Zura replied indignantly.

Cinder threw her hands in the air. "That's just it! You never pay me! And no matter how hard I work, I am always further away from paying off my debts than when I began!"

Zura rose smoothly from the floor and turned the ledger so the edges lined up with the table. "And you think living in some lice-infested hovel with a dozen other girls is a better alternative than one of the finest mansions in the city? And that's if some of them were even willing to take in a clanwoman."

"Mother—"

Zura slapped Cinder across the face. "Silence! You're lucky I don't send you the debtors' mine."

Resisting the urge to rub her cheek, Cinder lifted her chin. Because of the extreme danger of working in the cool bowels of the earth, which had become even more dangerous of late, the mines paid well. Better than Cinder could make as a simple house servant. "I would have to be two hundred attalics in debt before you could send me there. I'm sixty short."

An evil smile cracked Zura's face. "Are you?" She pulled a skeleton key from a long chain around her neck, inserted it into the one of the locks on the cabinet, and pulled open the door. In the cabinet, hundreds of jewels in elaborate settings glittered as if hungry for the light.

Zura gestured to a medium-sized trunk on the bottom shelf. "Magian, take this to the table." The girl hauled it from one of the shelves and set it down while Zura locked the cabinet. The key disappeared in the folds of her robe. She strode to the table and opened a chest. "Look inside."

Heart pounding with dread, Cinder took five hesitant steps to the table. Inside the chest were items of clothing made from rich linen, soft silks, and gauzy chiffons. She recognized them instantly.

Zura hauled out what had once been a teal overdress, clenching it in her fist. "After all I have done, you have repaid me by stealing?"

"I didn't steal it," Cinder began, "It was stained. My mother never wore—"

"Silence!" Zura threw the garment on the table. And grabbed another item. And another. And another. Seven pieces of clothing in all. All given to Cinder by companions who had cast them off. She had cut out the worn, stained fabric and pieced together what was left into something new. Something no one had ever seen—a fitted bodice and a skirt that flared out in the back, the front open to reveal the contrasting trousers beneath. It was feminine and practical.

"Sneaking, lock-picking, thieving, impudent child." Zura folded her arms across her chest and narrowed her gaze. "The value of those items is at least eighty attalics."

"Not even when the clothes were new!"

Zura slapped Cinder again. "Make a note in the ledger, Magian. Another eighty attalics. Which puts our dear Cinder at two hundred and twenty." Magian's quill scrapped across the vellum, forming ten elegant letters and numbers that damned Cinder.

Fighting a sick wave of fear, Cinder stood with her fists clenched, anger boiling inside her. She hadn't stolen, and the ruined clothing had had little to no value. But she was of clannish descent, which meant the courts would side with Zura.

Cinder closed her eyes, trying to count her breaths or the beat of her heart, but the numbers had abandoned her, turned against her. All she could see was the dark damp, the cold walls of the mines pressing in on her. It would be so much worse than the holding room in the cellar where Zura had sent her to be punished as a child. The cellar where she would sit in complete darkness, nothing to do but imagine the terrors crouching in the shadows. It was there Cinder learned the comfort of losing herself in the numbers.

"But then you may very well end up dead, and I would never see my money again." Zura let the last item of clothing slip from her fingers into a puddle of silk on the table. She meandered over to her cushions and lay back on them, then used a finger to trace patterns in the velvet. "I am merciful. Though you stole these garments, I can see the skill with which you reconstructed them."

Cinder felt a glimmer of hope. She had reworked the clothing at night, counting every stitch as her eyes strained in the dim light thrown by the oil lamps. She had taken the dresses to the city's tailors to show them her skill, but they had turned her away. Every single one.

Zura smoothed out the velvet and began drawing again. "So I will give you this chance you so desperately seek. Succeed, and you will become the seamstress for the House of Night. I will pay you one daric every three months, in addition to your room and board."

Cinder's mouth came open. A daric was a large gold coin, and what Zura offered was about double what the other tailors made. The numbers flooded Cinder's head. Her thumbs tapped against her fingertips, her mind spinning with calculations. She would be able to pay off her own debt in less than one year. Her mother and grandmother's debts in six. Seven more years—2,556 days—and they could *all* be free.

Zura smiled, showing perfectly straight teeth that gleamed, white and sharp. "We will place your creations on the new companion I plan to purchase. If she earns two hundred attalics in bids, you will begin the next day."

Cinder tipped her chin up. "What assurance do I have that you will keep your word?"

Zura waved her hand at her daughter. "Magian has already drawn up the contract."

Magian handed another scroll to Cinder, but aside from the numbers, the characters made little sense to her. Sweat broke out on her brow. Magian scooted next to her and began reading out loud, her voice as smooth and sure with the words as Cinder's fingers were with a needle.

Cinder held out her hand. "How do I know those are really the words Magian is reading?"

Annoyance flashed across Magian's face.

"Very well," Zura said with a sigh. "First thing tomorrow morning, you and I shall make a trip to the moneylender of your choosing. He or she can read the document and you can see for yourself."

Cinder considered the offer. Zura was a snake, but the woman wouldn't have anything to do with deciding Cinder's fate—that would now be decided by the patrons. And deep inside, Cinder knew the clothing she was making would be well received. "And if I fail?"

"Debtors' mine."

Cinder hesitated, knowing she couldn't trust Zura, yet also knowing she didn't have a choice.

"Make your decision, Cinder, for my mercy grows ever thinner."

Cinder pressed her lips together to keep her acid words from leaking out. Zura thought she would fail. But Cinder would show her. Clanwomen were strong as stone. More supple than a sapling. "I accept your bargain," Cinder said.

Zura watched her with emotionless eyes. "Tomorrow, after we visit the moneylenders, I will take you into the market and you will purchase whatever fabric you need. Be ready to leave first thing in the morning. If you can prove yourself worthy, the job will be yours."

Cinder felt the blood drain from her face. "You want me to purchase the material?"

Zura poured herself some more tea. "Of course, I will have to add it to your debt. If the companion proves worthy of my house, I will repay the cost of the material."

Cinder's gaze turned to the ledger, imagining the new numbers that would appear beneath her name. "You can't expect—"

"Are your dresses good enough, or aren't they?" Zura sipped her tea.

Cinder figured the numbers. The finest fabric and the best ornamentation would cost around forty attalics. Her total debt would still be well below the four hundred Zura needed to claim her as a slave. "My dresses are good enough."

Magian circled around the back of her table and placed the ledger in its cube. Sick to her stomach, Cinder turned toward the door. How was she ever going to tell her mother and grandmother what she'd just done?

"And Cinder," Zura called. Cinder paused, one hand stretched toward the door. "The outer gate is locked for a reason," the older woman finished. She called for Farush, who opened the door, cane in hand.

Cinder clenched her fists, her breaths coming hard and fast. But there was nothing to be done. She marched back into the room and lowered her robes. Standing naked from the waist up, she braced herself against the desk as the cane whipped through the air behind her.

CHAPTER TWO

Cinder was surrounded by colors. Hundreds of them, deep and rich, bright and airy, soft and subtle, bold and striking. The textures were nearly as varied. For once, she had no desire to count them. Instead, she could have spent hours sinking her hands into the plush fabrics, skimming her fingers across the slippery ones. But there wasn't time. Forcing herself to focus, she wandered through the aisles, searching for something that matched the vision in her head. Something that would look like lust-come-to-life under the lights.

And then she saw it. Wine-red, rich as blood. She touched the fabric, which shone like satin but was sturdier somehow, so it would hold her stitches without puckering. Cinder didn't know the name for the fabric—no one had ever taught her. But a name didn't matter, not when her hands knew by the feel and texture. She glanced at the price on the end of the bolt. Fingers tapping, she quickly calculated in her head. Six attalics. "I'll need a bolt of this one and another bolt of white," she said.

"Any other fabrics?" the girl asked.

Not yet, Cinder thought. *But soon.*

Where is this all being sent?" the apprentice cloth-maker asked sourly. This shop was the first place Cinder had come for a job months ago. Apparently, they wanted her shopping here only slightly more than they wanted her working here.

"The House of Night." Cinder started to move away to look over the threads when she saw three girls about her own age, all of them leaning close to listen. With the gold bedecking their bodies, and the three slaves trailing behind them carrying bolts of fabric, the girls were upper class.

"You're one of her companions, aren't you?" the lead girl said in disgust. Her eyes and forehead were wide, her chin narrow.

Growing up in a brothel, Cinder should have been used to this by now. Yet it never ceased to infuriate her. Right now she was a servant. But soon her gowns would be so well renowned that these girls would be begging for one.

She stared them down. "I am my own."

"Sadira." One of the other girls tugged on her arm. "Let's go."

"Why?" Sadira looked at her friend. "Afraid you'll catch something? You'd have to bed her for that." She snickered again.

Cinder deliberately turned her back on the girls and said to the apprentice, "I'll need matching thread as well." Only one-quarter of an attalic.

"Buttons or clasps?" the girl responded.

"Clasps—six of those antique gold ones you showed me earlier." Twelve attalics, but they would be worth it.

The girl nodded and started gathering up the order—eighteen attalics in as many minutes. It was enough to make Cinder sick. She watched to make sure the girl didn't cheat her.

"You can always tell a clanswoman," Sadira whispered loudly enough to be heard by the entire shop, "because they've had all the color washed out of them."

The welts on Cinder's back burned anew. She would not ruin her chance at freedom over this girl. She took a deep breath and counted doubles: *two, four, eight, sixteen, thirty-two, sixty-four . . .*

The apprentice looked nervously between Cinder and the other girls. "I can have everything delivered tonight."

"If you send one of your men, she can pay you from her bedroom," Sadira said. Her two friends burst into laughter.

Losing count, Cinder rounded on her and said, "Jealous that you can't even get a man to look at your goat face for free?" The moment the words left her lips, she wanted to snatch them back from the air. Not because she regretted them, but because she knew they would get her in trouble. Too late to worry about that now.

One of Sadira's friends snickered, and Sadira shot her a murderous glare.

Cinder turned on her heel and marched away without a backward glance. Sixteen steps later, she was outside the shop. The heat hit her. It was the hottest time of the year—the end of the dry season when the humidity had picked up but the rains hadn't cooled things off yet. She sagged against the stone wall and braced herself against her bent knees. She had to remember that while she might not be a slave, neither would she ever be those women's equal. They could mock her and bully her all they wanted. Fighting back would only make it worse.

She heard the girls coming her way, all indignation over her insult. Cinder hurried down the street. Maybe, just maybe, she would never see them again. Maybe Zura wouldn't hear of her insubordination. Counting her steps, Cinder broke into a run. She still had one stop to make before meeting up with Zura at her friend's house, and she was already behind schedule.

Holding her veil over her face to protect her pale skin from the relentless midmorning sun—and to hide her clannish features—Cinder crossed the dusty street and wove through the market of lesser goods. She kept her head down to hide her eyes, not wanting to elicit jeers or nasty glares, and picked up counting where she'd left off: *128, 256, 512 . . .*

When she reached the glassmakers' district, she stepped into the billowing heat of one of the finer shops. Forcing herself not to count the panes of glass waiting to be picked up, she made her inquiries. The master glassmaker wasn't too receptive at first. But once Cinder had convinced him she worked for the House of Night and had proven she could pay for half of her order up front, he reluctantly promised to try to make what she asked. One more stop at the cobblers, and then she was practically running back the way she'd come. She was supposed to meet the mistress at Tya's house long before now.

Cinder checked back over her numbers and started up where she'd left off: 1,024, 2,048, 4,098 . . . or was that 4,096? She was concentrating so deeply she didn't notice the girls from the cloth-maker's shop. Didn't see them as a pair of hands were planted firmly in her side, sending her sprawling into the path of an oncoming chariot. Cinder landed face first, her nose smacking the flagstones in a burst of pain. She looked up into the deep red of the horse's flared nostrils, its hooves poised to pound down on her. With no time to scramble out of the way, she curled into a ball and braced for impact, but the horse gathered itself on its hind legs and leapt over her. Two wheels churned as the chariot passed over her, the base of the axel scraping across the welts on her rounded shoulders.

Her back on fire, Cinder let out a breath. She felt warmth and wetness running down her chin, tasted blood, and realized her nose was bleeding under her veil. After unhooking it, she leaned forward so her blood would drip onto the dusty street instead of all over the front of her brown servant robes.

The driver hauled back on the reins and called out to the frightened horse, while another man leapt from the chariot, rushed to kneel beside Cinder, and pressed a bit of cloth to her face. "Are you all right?"

She tried to count the drops mixing with the dust beneath her, but quickly lost track in the mess. She gave a tight nod.

Rising to his feet, the man called out, "Sadira!"

The group of retreating girls froze. Sadira reluctantly turned her head, while the other girls stepped back from her as if she had some sort of disease. "Darsam, I didn't see you, my lord," she said.

Cinder's eyes widened. The House of Night was a hotbed of gossip, and the wild son of the city lord featured in many of those stories. It was purported that Darsam ran his own gang of tribesmen thieves, and because of the connection with his father, the city watch was powerless to do anything to stop him.

Darsam's fists were clenched, his jaw tight. Slowly, as if by force of will, the tension drained out of him, and he affected a careless stance—eight fingers tucked under his folded arms. "Haven't you heard? Murder is punishable by instant beheading in Idara."

The girl's gaze slid to the side, searching the shadows between buildings as if for help. No help came. Sadira straightened. "You can't murder a slave. Only put them down like a dirty animal."

The man's gaze shifted down to Cinder. She shot to her feet, blood running down her face, and yanked off her headscarf to reveal the cobalt tattoos on her scalp above her ear. "I am no slave."

Sadira's face paled. "Well—she's still clannish. And a whore."

"I am not a whore! And unfortunately, I'm not clannish either." The last bit she said under her breath.

Sadira faltered for a moment and then visibly braced herself. "You come from the House of Night, do you not?"

Cinder couldn't deny it. "I'm a servant there."

Sadira narrowed her gaze, hate spitting from her eyes. "Liar."

Cinder spit blood into the dirt. "You're just mad I called you goat-face. But really, it's your parents you should be angry with. I had nothing to do with it."

The girl's eyes narrowed, hatred rolling off her. Beside her, Darsam snorted. Then he was laughing. Sadira's hateful gaze transferred to him.

Still grinning, he swept his gaze over Cinder, lingering a beat on the blond hair settled around her shoulders. He was perhaps a handful of years older than her seventeen, and his dark chest was bare to the unforgiving sun. But instead of a shaved head and long beard, his face was clean shaven, and black curls framed his face. Cinder made the mistake of looking into his eyes—black like the strongest orray and lined with kohl. She could have sworn she saw admiration in their depths.

He was beautiful, she realized. Beautiful and powerful— two things that made him very dangerous for her. She tore her gaze away, tapping her thumb to her fingers to distract her from the disconcerting warmth spreading through her.

"I've done nothing wrong," Sadira insisted.

The man's admiration shuttered off, leaving behind a dark rage he fastened on Sadira. "And what about my chariot? Or my horses? My team is the best in the province. One of them could have broken a leg."

Sadira shifted her weight uncertainly. "They didn't."

"Even whores have rights," Darsam said.

"I'm sure you know all about whores and their rights," Sadira snapped. "Why don't you pay her a visit later? Check for injuries yourself." She sent a scathing glance back into the shadows, whirled around, and stormed down the street. Her friends didn't follow.

Cinder spit blood onto a flagstone and did her best to wipe her face clean with her sleeve. "I'm not a whore." She wasn't sure if she was shaking from indignation or shock or both.

Darsam's gaze was steady. "I haven't anything against whores."

She whipped around, glaring at him for the insult she was sure he'd just given her. But movement behind him drew her attention. A figure in black, wearing a veil. His gaze locked with Cinder's, and her mouth came open in a silent gasp. She recognized those close-set eyes—the man carting the piss pots. The one who'd spied on her for Zura, and who was probably spying on her now.

Darsam pivoted to see what she was looking at. But the piss-pot man was already moving away. "Who was that?" Darsam asked.

Cinder forced herself to remember who this was—the lord's son. She counted down from ten and then back up again before she trusted herself to speak. "I have to meet the mother." Without another word, she turned on her heel and started down the street.

"Wait," he called after her. "What's your name?"

She didn't slow.

"I command it," Darsam said, his voice ringing.

Cinder paused, fury coursing through her in waves. She could feel the watching Idarans' gazes boring into her—two by two by two. A lord's son could make unending amounts of trouble for her. Better to give him what he wanted rather than raise his ire. "Cinder," she said before gathering her robes into her hands and running down the street.

When she arrived at Zura's friend's house, Cinder was breathless, having paused only long enough to wash her face and as much of her robes as she could in a nearly dried-out public fountain. This neighborhood had been fine once, but now chunks of plaster had fallen from the walls, and some of the shutters were missing.

Cinder slipped passed Zura's guards, who smoked idly by the chariot, and passed through the little gate into the courtyard that used to hold flowers. Now there were fifteen rows of vegetables and twelve sapling fruit trees. Cinder knocked on the faded turquoise door with its chipped mermaid knocker. A moment later, a slave girl with the dark skin and tightly curling hair of the Luathan opened the door. Cinder entered the house, and the girl quickly shut the door behind her. The thick planks were designed to keep the heat out for as long as possible.

It took a moment for Cinder's eyes to adjust to the dimness. The anteroom was meticulously clean, but some of the marble tiles were cracked, and the furnishings were a little sparse and worn.

Without saying a word, the slave girl led Cinder to the tea room. It was small and rather dim, with the shutters firmly closed against the sun. In the center of the room were cushions of purple velvet that had once been fine but now bore the permanent impressions of numerous rumps. Zura sat with her friend, Tya. The woman used to own the Star, one of the finer pleasure houses in the university district. But that was before it went bankrupt nearly a year ago.

Cinder slipped quietly into the room. While she waited to be acknowledged, she started counting the pearls struggling to escape the rolls of fat around Tya's neck: *one, two, three, four, five, six.*

A little older than Zura, Tya gazed at the swirling dust motes caught in the shafts of light leaking through the shutters. "I think what I miss more than anything is the dancing." The woman sounded constantly breathless. Her jowls jiggled as she spoke, making it even more challenging to keep track of the pearls. "The Star was renowned for it above all else. Patrons would come from all over the city to see my girls dance."

Zura sipped her tea. "I remember."

Seven, eight, nine . . .

"I shall stop by tomorrow," Tya wheezed. "I would like to see the dancing again."

Zura set her tea cup on the tray. "I'm afraid that isn't possible."

The woman straightened up indignantly. "Why ever not?"

Ten, eleven, twelve, thirteen . . .

"It wouldn't be good for my house."

"But I've come since the Star went out of business. Why would that—" Tya's gaze turned shrewd. "Oh, Zura, he got to you too."

Zura stiffened. "I don't know what you're talking about."

Fourteen, fifteen, sixteen, seventeen . . .

"You'd be better off to sell now." Tya coughed, phlegm rattling in her throat. "All of it. Take what you can and retire. Before he owns all of it."

Cinder was so distracted she lost count of the pearls altogether. She wondered what the two women were talking about. Surely Zura wasn't in any financial duress. It was rumored that she had more jewels than the queen herself. It was also said that the meals the patrons ate were finer than what was served in the palace.

Zura gathered her robes to stand. "The House of Night is the greatest pleasure house in all of Idara. It will—"

"Not if Bahar has his say. And he will."

What does the false lord have to do with anything? Cinder wondered.

"If the brothels go down," Zura went on as she pushed to her feet, "the slaves are only a step behind. Then we'll both be out of business. It's in Jatar's best interest that we both flourish."

Cinder knew that name—Jatar was a leader of the slaver's guild, one of the richest men in Idara.

Tya struggled to stand, and for a moment the pearls disappeared altogether. "He's like a hyena on carrion, snapping the bones to suck out the marrow before the carcass turns to dust." Cinder shivered through the heat prickling her skin.

"It may be some time before I can visit again." Zura turned on her heel and started at the sight of Cinder. "How long have you been spying there?"

She tried to appear innocent. "I only just walked in, Mother."

Zura took hold of her arm and hauled her toward the door even as Tya waddled after them. "You're late. Again. Apparently twenty lashings wasn't enough to impress upon you the importance of punctuality."

"I was . . . delayed." Cinder's fingers started tapping at the thought of Sadira and her taunts. Of Darsam and his commands.

As the slave girl hurried to open the door for them, Zura really looked at Cinder. The older woman's eyes widened. "Your robes are covered in blood. What happened?"

Cinder tapped faster. "A girl named Sadira."

Zura looked back to find Tya watching them, arms straining to fold across her ample chest. "Not another word," Zura said under her breath as she strode outside, the door closing softly behind them.

As soon as they were on the other side of the low wall, Zura pulled Cinder around and studied her face. "There's no damage." She relaxed a little and hauled Cinder into the chariot, the guards a couple of steps behind them. Zura picked up the reins and slapped them across the horse's back. No one besides herself could ever drive a chariot to her satisfaction. They lurched onto the street. "Tell me *exactly* what happened."

When Cinder finished with the story, Zura had pursed her thin lips into an even thinner line. "Darsam is one of Lord Bahar's younger sons. He's wild and willful. And you say he showed interest in you? How much interest?"

Cinder shrugged, then wished she hadn't as it pulled at the welts on her back. "He said he liked whores."

Zura's eyes spun with scheming. "Perhaps the House of Night shall send a personal invitation to the auction for this Darsam."

"The false lord's son?" Farood spat in disgust.

"He's not even an Idaran. Fool tribesman knows nothing about running a city," Farush added.

Cinder hated tribesmen almost as much as she hated Idarans. She'd been a child during the Clan War. She remembered cowering in the dark tunnels beneath the winter palace in Idara, hoping the clanmen would beat down the doors and set her family free. Instead, the tribesmen had given the city aid. Queen Nelay had become a goddess and driven the clanmen out in a storm of fire and ash.

In return for their aid, the tribesmen had been given lordships over all Idara's cities. But instead of being grateful, the Idarans hated them for it—for their strict ways and sticky honor. And the fact that over the last decade, Bahar's new tariffs had shut down much of the once-thriving pleasure and slave guilds.

Zura shot Cinder a cunning smile. "If Darsam finds our establishment favorable, the tribesmen lords may follow. And if enough men of power return as our patrons, Bahar will have to back down."

The two thugs' heads came up. They nodded in approval.

"And the girl?" Zura asked Cinder. "What was her name again?"

Cinder's nose and the welts on her back seemed to throb all the more. "Sadira."

Zura's gaze narrowed. "Ah, I remember now. Daughter to the leader of the silver miners' guild—one of Ash's patrons."

No wonder Sadira hated any woman who came from the House of Night—her father was one of Ash's patrons. At nearly forty-seven, Cinder's mother still looked to be in her thirties. And she still had enough loyal patrons to remain a companion.

To Cinder's surprise, Zura didn't turn up the rise toward the mansion, but instead wove down twenty-seven streets to the poorer sections of town. Cinder watched as the buildings became more dilapidated, the people more ragged. Seven naked children played in filthy puddles in the street. The gloriously painted and carved doors that Idarans so prided themselves on became warped and rough, with paint chips of multiple colors embedded deep in the grain.

The chariot headed down a mean-looking street. A pair of thugs guarding the entrance to an alley looked over their shoulders at Zura and nodded before turning their backs. When Zura turned the chariot up that alley, Cinder couldn't stop staring. Men and women lined the broken flagstone street. All of them were naked, save for a thin loincloth.

Cinder knew the story, though her grandmother Storm had told it only once. Of standing naked under the relentless sun with her suckling baby in her arms. Of the men parading past her, touching her, inspecting her teeth. Of a language she barely understood, spoken fast and loud. And then she had come to live in the mansion and become a companion.

Zura dropped from the chariot and paced forward, her guards a step behind her. "Cinder," she called in exasperation. "Must I beat you to get you to keep up?"

Dozens of finely dress Idarans, all of them reeking of money, turned to consider Cinder as if she too might be for sale. Counting her steps, she rushed to catch up to the mistress as they strode past a line of slave men. Some were muscular and strong, others old and withered. There were children, too. Weeping children. Most of them looked like Cinder—pale, blue-eyed, blond. They were clansmen and women—her people—though there were some Luathans with charcoal skin and tightly curled hair. Cinder counted her steps so she wouldn't have to meet their gazes. She'd never been so glad to be freeborn.

"Where are we going, Mother?" she asked pleadingly.

Not bothering to answer, Zura stepped before a door featuring a carving of a grotesque face with distorted features. As the older woman straightened her veil, Cinder noticed her hands shaking, almost as if she were nervous. What could possibly make Zura nervous?

Cinder took three smaller steps so the number of steps would be an even sixty. Farood knocked, and a man who was missing half his teeth pushed open the door, releasing the smell of human waste and sweat mingled with a sickeningly sweet perfume. Cinder tied up her blood-stained veil and breathed shallowly.

Holding a scented handkerchief under her nose, Zura, along with the guard, disappeared inside the darkness beyond. Cinder didn't want to go in there—didn't want to see what awaited her. But then a muffled scream rose up behind her. She started and hurried the six steps after Zura. Inside was some kind of anteroom cloaked in shadows. A toothless guard stared at Cinder and Zura. More guards were posted at the entrance to each corridor.

To keep the slaves from escaping, Cinder realized. She tried to remember how many steps she'd taken since coming inside to add it to her total, but her mind was blank and panicked. She forced herself to concentrate. And the number came suddenly—sixty-six.

One of the guards called out, "Durux."

A moment later a man emerged from the dark corridor. His gaze flicked to Cinder, though he didn't meet her gaze. He was

AMBER ARGYLE

perhaps a few years older than her, whip thin, with large ears framing a lumpy, bald head covered in swirls of tattoos that almost made her dizzy. He smiled an oily smile. "Zura, if you will follow me."

They started down the long corridor to a door—sixteen steps, bringing Cinder's total to eighty-two. Durux gestured for them to enter. Zura looked back at Cinder. "Wait here." She straightened her robes, then she and the guards stepped inside, leaving Cinder with the bald man who stared at her body as if he was trying to see inside it. Cinder closed her eyes, her lips working as she counted: *seven, fourteen, twenty-eight, fifty-six . . .*

"Jatar," Zura said from behind her handkerchief, "I see you received my message to view your new stock."

Before Cinder could hear anymore, Durux shut the door.

One hundred twelve, two hundred twenty-four, four hundred forty-eight . . .

"You're Zura's freeborn girl, Cinder." The way he said her name—like he was tasting it—made her shudder.

She looked a little closer and noticed his close-set eyes. "You're the one who's been following me!"

In front of her, the door opened to a barrel-chested and finely dressed man probably in his mid-forties. A sparkling ring adorned each of his fingers. Squinting at Cinder as if he couldn't see very well, he reached out and undid her veil before she could react. He studied her in the way a man might look at a horse he was thinking of buying. "So this is the girl who's caused you so much trouble," he said to Zura.

The mistress crossed her arms over her small chest. "She has nothing to do with this, Jatar."

"Oh, I think she has everything to do with it." Jatar stepped aside and motioned for Cinder to come in. Wanting desperately to run away, she glanced back down the corridor. There stood

Durux, his face in shadow. Eighty-two steps past three guards and an alley full of slaves, buyers, and slave drivers.

Cinder stepped into the room and gasped at the lavishness of the decor. Eight gold cushions surrounded one table and a deep-red mosaic floor, the tiles of which she was itching to count. But the beauty was spoiled by twelve naked girls lined up along one wall, their dark skin oiled and buffed to a shine. They were all Luathan, their tightly curled hair braided or rolled together like rope.

From behind, Jatar rolled a lock of Cinder's hair between his fingers. She spun around and batted his hand away. He stepped back as a grin overtook his face. "Well, she's certainly beautiful enough for it. But she has not the desire to please. Of course, some men like that."

Thinking of Durux, Cinder moved back three steps, her gaze going between Jatar and Zura. "What's going on, Mother?"

Ignoring her, the mistress told Jatar, "You let me take care of that."

"You sure this is the gambit you're willing to take?" he asked.

Zura's chin came up. "You said it yourself. People are like fields—you have to sow before you can reap."

Jatar rolled his eyes. "As long as I get my money."

Cinder didn't know what was going on, but she had a sinking feeling it had something to do with her. "I'm not for sale."

He studied her. "Everyone is for sale. You just have to know the price." He pushed past her, his shoulder bumping her out of the way.

Tapping her fingers to her thumb, Cinder glared after him. She would never be a companion.

Zura's gaze raked the slaves, starting with a young girl with budding breasts, all the way to a woman with gorgeous curves. And Cinder understood. These slaves would not be auctioned off before the masses like the rest. No, these were reserved for men who had the money to pay for pleasures. Cinder shuddered with revulsion.

"These are the best?" Zura asked Jatar.

Still squinting, he stepped up beside her and pointed. "These three can sing. The middle five are fair dancers. All can serve and act when they have to—I made sure of that. The one on the end hasn't the talent for either, but with her body, who cares." He was referring to the woman with the generous curves.

Zura rounded on Cinder. "Tell me, which would you choose?"

Disgusted, Cinder cleared her throat and looked up from counting tiles—she'd already reached twenty-eight. "Mother?"

The woman sighed. "You wish to be my seamstress, which means you will be in charge of making these women beautiful. You have more to lose than I do. Tell me, which one would you choose?"

Cinder knew she was being punished for sneaking out. For wanting something more. She wanted to turn around and leave the room. But she knew the stakes. If she didn't take this chance, she'd wind up in the mines. When she returned, no one would hire her, and she'd end up in a common brothel. She took a hesitant step forward. Pretending the girls were dress forms, she covered them with cloth in dozens of colors, concealing their faults and enhancing their strengths. She imagined the way the girls would look under the lights as they danced. And she realized what would probably come after that dance.

"I can't," she whispered.

Zura's hand came up hard and fast, leaving Cinder's cheek stinging. "You think it a burden to be one of my girls? The House of Night is the finest in Idara. Any girl who is chosen will live in luxury. My girls are well treated, and I do not allow abuse from their clients—which is more than I can say for the lives that await every other girl here. The false lord thinks he's freeing whores, but he's really just forcing them to live in the back rooms or shadows of the taverns or alleyways."

Cinder's cheek still stung as she started counting tiles again. Zura paced up and down the line of slaves. "It doesn't matter," she said finally. "With the right makeup and clothes, I can make any of them beautiful. With the right attitude, I can make any of them desirable. It's talent that makes a woman stand out."

She stopped before the last girl, who looked no more than twelve. She was pretty, with startlingly large eyes framed by thick lashes, and a nose dusted with freckles. Cinder thought she almost looked like a frightened kitten.

"You said this one can sing?" Zura asked. At Jatar's nod, she announced, "I'll take her." The older woman's eyes glittered with malice as she turned to Cinder. "And you will teach her."

Cinder's head snapped up. "What?"

"You have the most stake in her success, do you not?"

Cinder's heart sank as she stared at the girl. Barely more than a child, she seemed fragile somehow. Of all the slaves, Cinder thought, this one was the least likely to be chosen by Zura. The one least likely to earn enough bids to become a companion. Zura was counting on Cinder failing! But she wouldn't.

"I'm not the one wasting my money by buying her," Cinder said sullenly.

Zura slapped her again. This time, Cinder barely felt the sting. "You know so little about the lusts of men," the older woman said. "But you're about to learn." She turned to Jatar. "Twenty attalics."

"I can get twenty-five from any of these lords," he shot back.

"Yes, but they'll only buy from you once, maybe twice. I buy from you every year, so I get first pick and a better price."

Jatar made a growling sound low in his throat. "You forget who's loaning you the money."

She waved his comment away. "You'll get it back by week's end, and you know it. Twenty two."

Zura's conversation with Tya snapped into place in Cinder's mind. Zura was in debt to Jatar, but the woman was somehow convinced she would have the money in a few days. Did Zura really think this little Luathan girl would fetch enough bids to get her out of debt? Cinder was ashamed to admit that the idea gave her a queasy sort of hope. Maybe she could make something of this girl after all.

The door suddenly came open, sending a breeze through the room that set the lamps to flickering. Shadows danced across Zura's and Jatar's faces as if the light was afraid to touch them. Durux strolled in and stood beside the older man. "You're needed."

Jatar growled in displeasure and turned back to Zura. "Twenty-two. Now get out."

Zura gave a curt nod. "Have her delivered to the mansion." She turned on her heel and started for the door.

Cinder made to follow and then looked back. Durux had the girl trapped between the wall and himself, though no part of him touched her. He breathed deeply, obviously savoring the smell of her as his nose moved down her neck and followed her collarbone. "We didn't have a chance to play, little kitten."

"Leave her alone." Cinder was shocked at the words whipping from her mouth like a lash.

Durux's dark eyes snapped up to catch Cinder. "Oh, but I have left her alone. He made me promise I would." The backs of his fingers stroked the girl's cheek.

Cinder shot a look down the hall—at Zura's retreating form, and Jatar ahead of her—and called loudly, "How will your patrons feel about your slaves being tainted?"

"Durux!" Jatar shouted without turning back. "Do we have to have another conversation?"

Durux slinked away from the slave, his gaze hot on Cinder as he stepped toward her. "Why didn't you just say you wanted to play too?" He reached for her arm, but she jerked back.

"Don't touch me."

Farush and Farood appeared out of nowhere, and Cinder had never been so appreciative of their presence.

Durux let out a long sigh. "I do so hate the rules of this game. But if I must play, I play to win."

He cast a mournful look at the slave girl and then slunk down the hall. Once he was out of sight, Cinder sagged, all the fight draining out of her.

"I don't like him," Farush said.

"Sick, twisted little beggar," Farood agreed. Such disgust from one such as Farood was telling. He looked down at Cinder, his expression a fraction softer. "Come along, for the mother loses her patience."

Glancing back at the crying slave, Cinder suddenly felt glad the girl was coming to the House of Night. Ludicrous as it sounded, she would be safer in a companion house than with these slavers. Cinder grasped for the numbers. She was too rattled for doubles, so she settled on counting her steps—eighty-two of them from this horrible place and back to the chariot.

CHAPTER THREE

The girl was crying, one shuddering breath for every three hiccupping sobs. Cinder concentrated on the numbers to keep herself from losing control. She kept reminding herself that she was fine—she wasn't being locked up. No good reason existed for the panic reaching up from her stomach to choke her throat and make it difficult to breath. No reason to want to whirl and run for it.

Zura slipped the skeleton key from around her neck and inserted it into the door. She waited for Farush and Farood to enter the cell and then followed. Cinder took firm hold of the tray and stepped into the dank room, which had been built into the cellar. The slave girl darted to her feet, her fists clenched around the gray sack she wore.

Zura tucked the key into her robes. "You will work hard," she told the girl. "You will improve. And if not, you will be punished. Am I clear?"

The silence stretched out. "Yes," the girl said finally, her voice grating as if she hadn't spoken in days.

Zura's hand snaked out and slapped her hard. "Yes, *Mother*," Zura corrected.

The girl staggered back, a welt in the shape of a hand print forming on her cheek. "Yes, Mother." Cinder could hear more of an accent this time. The girl's "th" almost sounded like "d."

Zura nodded. "Good. Your name is now Naiba. Eat and then Cinder will begin teaching you."

"Surely one of the companions would be more suitable," Cinder said morosely. "One of the women from the Luathan section—they know their people's dances and songs better than I do."

Zura whirled on her. "If this girl fails, so do you. You have seen the dances and heard the songs all your life. If you're not clever enough to know them by now, you have no place in my household." She pushed past Cinder, her feet making measured clipping sounds—*one-two, one-two*—that slowly faded as she started up the stairs that led out of sight.

Cinder closed her eyes. *I am not locked up, I am not locked up, I am not locked up. Zura is trying to make me fail. She wants me in the debtors' mine.* Cinder turned to face the girl, who stared silently back, tears streaming down her face. She would never do as a companion, even if she could sing.

"My name is Cinder. I wasn't sure how well they were feeding you before." Cinder settled the tray by the blankets and hoped the girl didn't notice her shaking hands. "So I brought something easy on the stomach—broth and bread."

Naiba stared hungrily at the tray. She resisted a moment then plopped down, picked up the bowl, and drank straight through. She tore off a chunk of bread and finished it in nine bites. "You have an Idaran mark?" she said, her tone almost accusatory.

Cinder winced. She knew what the girl really meant. Cinder was clearly clannish, so why the Idaran tattoo? "I was born here," she answered, "so I'm free. My mother is clannish. I don't know my father." He could be one of dozens of men, none of whom had ever laid claim to Cinder, but she wouldn't tell Naiba that.

"I wonder if my parents know what happened to me," the girl said. "I was fishing when they stole me."

Cinder tried to harden herself to the words, knowing this would be easier if she didn't get attached. Attachments in the House of Night usually led to pain.

After she downed the last of her bread, the girl asked in a low voice, "What will happen to me?"

Cinder hesitated before deciding she would rather know the truth if she were in Naiba's place. "Your skills as a performer will be auctioned off—you will be hired out as an entertainer. After you've gained some notoriety, your virginity will be auctioned off as well. The highest bidders will have access to your bed, but I'm sure Zura won't expect that from you until you're older—probably around seventeen. The more money you earn, the more lavish and comfortable your life. The less you earn . . ." Cinder didn't finish.

The girls eyes slipped closed as a horrified shudder tore through her. She shot Cinder a disgusted look. "You're free to do anything you want, and you chose *this*?"

"I don't have a choice." Cinder picked up the tray and marched out the door, not caring if Naiba followed. "How am I ever supposed to reach two hundred attalics in bids on a girl the men can't even bed?" Cinder muttered to herself.

Six steps to cross the cellar, filled with fruits grown in the Hansi Province, and half of a sheep carcass. Twelve simple wooden stairs and she stepped into the kitchen. The air was heavy with the smell of roast lamb and cinnamon. Cinder paused, counting to five for each breath, in and out, until her heart stopped racing.

Storm, her grandmother, was busy preparing breakfast in the outdoor ovens. She had aged out and come to work as a cook. At forty-seven, Cinder's mother wasn't far off from being retired as a companion, though there were rumors that one of her patrons wanted to purchase her—something Cinder refused to think about.

Scattered throughout the kitchen, six companion children peeled and sliced and kneaded in preparation for dinner. Their mothers were slaves, just like Cinder's mother. They were all in debt, same as Cinder, though she was by far the oldest.

Naiba cast a longing glance at the food. Cinder didn't bother. Servants would eat whatever was left over. If there was anything. "This is where the servants and slaves prepare the food," she explained. "After the companions and their patrons eat, it's our turn."

Naiba glanced at the strong light trailing through the open door. "Isn't it a little late for breakfast?"

"The House of Night has late hours," Cinder replied. She crossed the kitchen in sixteen steps and wound up twenty circular stairs to the second-floor attic. Inside were two rows of sixteen blankets where the servants slept. Nearest the far window was Cinder's space—a couple of worn blankets and the few treasures she had managed to collect over the years. A comb with most of the teeth broken off, a shard of a mirror, a few interesting rocks, and some pretty scraps of material. There was also a dress form she had made herself, stuffing the worn linen with threadbare rags and mounting it to an old broom handle.

She stopped before some clean bedding and an empty basket waiting to hold Naiba's things, not that the slave girl had any. "You'll stay here until you've earned your title as companion. It's unbearably hot in the evenings and cold by morning, but you sort of get used to it."

Naiba looked it over and said softly, "I used to share my bed with my sisters—there are five of us. We didn't have any brothers. My father always said he was cursed with girls, but he always smiled when he said it so we knew he didn't mean anything by it."

Cinder had never known a father—never known a man's love. All she knew from the House of Night was that men were never to be trusted, only subtly manipulated. Outright manipulation was only done by the men.

Twelve steps later, Cinder stood before the narrow window and motioned for Naiba to look out. From their place atop the rise, they could see the city spread out before them. The lord's palace rose up on their right. Each district in the city had its own pleasure house, though many of them were boarded up now.

Below the window, the courtyard was covered in flowers. Cinder's gaze lingered on one plant in particular. It wasn't especially pretty, but its earthy, clean scent drifted up to the window at night, reminding Cinder of Holla, her aunt buried beneath it. Clanwomen were always buried, unlike Idarans, whose custom was to burn their dead.

"The mansion is inside a walled compound near the lord's palace," Cinder told Naiba. "The gates are locked, and Zura will beat you if you try to escape." Even as she said it, she fingered the lock-picking tools hidden beneath her breast wrap. It would be fairly easy to set the girl free. But even if Cinder did, where would Naiba go? No one in the city would help her. On the contrary, she'd be turned in to the city watch and returned, probably before morning. And then she and Cinder would be beaten so badly they wouldn't be able to walk for a week.

"Not to mention the guard," Naiba commented.

Startled, Cinder looked closer and saw a man sitting in the shadows of the trees near the gate. One guard, one cudgel . . . zero chance of making a run for it.

"Come on, let's get started." Cinder pulled out her measuring tape and memorized the girl's measurements. For a while, her mind was lost to the efficiency and order of the numbers. While she worked, she told Naiba the house rules, which basically boiled down to doing as they were told, always referring to

Zura as "Mother," and remembering that she had spies among the companions, slaves, and servants. It was best not to speculate on who those spies might be, as they tended to shift when Zura had something to blackmail one of them with.

"Why does she want us to call her "Mother"?" Naiba asked.

Cinder tapped her fingers in ascending order. *One, two, three, four. Four, three, two, one.* "Because that's how she sees herself."

"It's a lie." Naiba turned angry eyes to Cinder. "A mother wants what's best for her children. Not what's best for herself."

"Don't let anyone else hear you say that."

Footsteps pounded up the stairs. Cinder gave Naiba a pointed look before a breathless Marish appeared in the doorway and reported, "Storm says to get the serving done before you're late."

Pursing her lips, Cinder hustled back downstairs. Naiba trailed behind her. At the table, the girls were already plating the flatbread. Lugging a pot of khash—sheep's head, brains, hooves, garlic, lemon slices, and cinnamon cooked through the night—Storm pushed into the kitchen. She set the pot on the long table and used her shoulder to wipe the sweat from her face. Nearly in her seventies, she was a beautiful woman, with wavy silver hair that matched her silver eyes and gently seamed skin.

"This is the little slip that Mother spent her money on?" Storm growled.

Knowing Storm was frustrated that her granddaughter still hadn't found a job, Cinder shrugged. "She can sing. Zura put me in charge of teaching her."

"You?" Storm exclaimed. "Why? You're not one of her companions, and who's going to do your serving?"

Cinder gave another shrug. "The other girls will have to manage. I have a dress to make before the auction in three days."

"No. You will serve and clean, as you always do." Cinder turned at the new voice, surprised to find Magian standing in the doorway.

Cinder sputtered, "But how am I to prepare Naiba if I still have all my work to do?"

Magian entered the room and gathered the breakfast tray. "You managed to traipse all over the city looking for a job and sew a dozen dresses. Compared to that, this shouldn't be too hard. Now, move to it. Or I'll be forced to tell my mother." She turned on her heel and left.

"Seven," Cinder muttered under her breath. "It was seven dresses." She balanced five trays, two on each arm and one on her head. "You might as well see the mansion," she told Naiba. "Bring a tray with you."

The girl stuck to Cinder's side as she hurried outdoors. The other children followed, carrying their own trays. Fifteen steps through a long colonnade that led to the main building. Thirty-eight thick stone columns decorated in beautiful tile mosaics made up the interior. Between columns was a pivot door that could be opened to let in the heat, or closed to keep it out. This time of year, the doors stood open to catch the morning breeze off the river that carved a fat brown path through the verdant valley. It wouldn't be long before the monsoons came, flooding the river into a lake that would feed the rich fields. The building itself featured glittering marble floors, and ceilings resplendent with mosaics of circles within circles.

The group broke apart, two girls each starting for one of four wings housing twelve companions each. Cinder headed to the clanswomen section. Here, the walls were made of what looked like stones rounded from the relentless rushing of a clean river, but were really just plaster. Murals featured high mountains capped in white and green forests and fields. A poor substitute for the real thing, Cinder's grandmother always said.

Not hearing Naiba's steps behind her, Cinder carefully turned back to see the girl moving in a slow circle, her mouth hanging open.

"Keep up," Cinder said. With a start, the girl ran after her, porcelain ratting dangerously. "Be care—" Cinder began even as she backpedaled. But it was too late. The girl slipped on the smooth marble. Cinder watched as one teapot, one cup, one saucer, one bowl of khash, and one plate of flatbread came crashing down. Five things, shattered into dozens.

"Stupid girl! Do you know how much that will cost me?" In her head, Cinder calculated the amount Zura would deduct from her pay.

Naiba winced as if Cinder had slapped her. "I'm sorry."

How was Cinder ever going to make this child into a performer so awe-inspiring that men would pay handsomely for her presence at their meetings? Cinder closed her eyes, counting doubles: *132, 264, 528.* Calmer now, she let out a long sigh. "I'm so far in debt at this point, what's three more attalics. Gather everything onto the tray. Hurry back to the kitchen, fetch another tray and bring it to me. Then you'll have to hurry back and clean this up. The men will start to filter down any moment, and we can't allow them to see such a mess."

She hurried away without waiting to see if Naiba would obey. Cinder already risked another caning for being so behind schedule. She bypassed the great room with its center platform, banquet tables, and low tables surrounded with purple-and-gold velvet. At this time of day, the bedrooms, located on the building's periphery, were closed tight, since most of the occupants still slept.

Cinder went from one room's antechamber to another. She settled the plates on the small table, rang a bell to wake the companions and their patrons in adjacent bedrooms, and left to go to the next room. Cinder always saved her mother's for last—

luckily Naiba had finally caught up with a tray when she reached it. As usual, Ash waited at her small table.

Cinder quickly introduced Naiba to her mother and then sent the younger girl back to clean up her mess. After shutting the door behind her, Cinder settled the tray down and kissed her mother's smooth cheek. Her golden hair and silver eyes still made her a favorite among the older patrons.

"Did you manage to find a job?" Ash spoke softly, as she always did in her rooms, for they never knew who was listening through the seven peepholes they'd found in the walls. Not to mention the fact that Ash's patron was still asleep in the bedroom.

Counting as she set out the dishes, Cinder wondered if she should tell her mother about the deal she'd made with Zura. But there was nothing to be done about it now, and talking about it would only upset her mother.

Unfortunately, Ash was quite perceptive. She took Cinder's calloused hands in her soft ones and said, "I've heard that Mubia is more open to those with clannish blood. Perhaps you should go there to seek a job."

"Zura would never let me leave the city. Not with my debts." Cinder didn't say the rest. Zura was convinced Cinder would be on the first ship to the clanlands, never to look back, even though Cinder had no intention of ever leaving her mother and grandmother behind.

Ash sighed. "Pour the hot water." She went to a side table and removed the lid to a little jar. Here was the safest place to talk, since the bedroom was on the other side and no one could read their lips to tell they were whispering—something strictly forbidden. Ash pulled out three leaves of the wedlock weed that would keep her from having a child. Cinder brought her a cup and stood so their shoulders were touching.

Ash set the leaves in the sieve to steep. As the bitter steam wafted up, she met Cinder's gaze. "Who is the new Luathan?"

Cinder bit the inside of her cheek. "A slave Zura is putting up for auction."

Ash's brow furrowed. "Then why is she with the servants and not being trained by the Luathan companions?"

Cinder tried to think of a way out of telling her mother the truth, then finally said, "I'm to teach her."

Her mother removed the leaves, stirred honey into the tea, and took a sip of her tea, and made a face at the bitter taste. "There's something you're not telling me."

Cinder sighed. "Zura offered me a job as the House of Night's seamstress."

Ash set down her teacup. "And you agreed?"

"I didn't have a choice. Zura found the dresses I've been making. She accused me of stealing. It was agree to be her seamstress or go to the debtors' mine." Cinder shuddered at the thought. "I made her sign a contract. The moneychangers read it aloud to me."

"Contract or not, you can't trust Zura or her promises. Cinder, we have to get you out of here."

She felt the old panic rising up within her. "I can't leave you and Grandmother."

Her mother took hold of her arm, fingernails digging in—a reminder to keep her voice down. "Listen to me. You—"

Her words cut off as the bedroom door opened. Wearing his sleep clothes, General Balthdur grinned at Ash. He was the main reason she hadn't been retired yet; he was negotiating with Zura to purchase Ash as soon as his ailing wife died. Cinder couldn't look at the man without wanting to strangle his fat neck.

"What are you two whispering about, my clanwoman?" Two arms snaked around Cinder's mother from behind. Ash shot Cinder a fierce look that sent her scampering for the door. She closed it softly behind her, blocking out the wet sounds of their kissing.

Cinder had spent too long in her mother's rooms. Already some men were in the corridors, reminding each other of the drunken business deals they'd made the night before—her grandmother often said the entire province was run from this brothel. Cinder kept her head down, moving smoothly to attract as little attention as possible. Still, she felt more than one pair of eyes following her.

CHAPTER FOUR

If she couldn't sew, Cinder decided she could at least train Naiba while she cleaned. On her hands and knees, Cinder counted strokes as she scrubbed the tile floor near the banquet tables. Naiba stood at the exact center of the platform like she was afraid the walls might collapse in on her. For the fourth time, Cinder stopped scrubbing to show her the Luathan dances. Soap bubbles dripped down her arms as she demonstrated the elegant curls and turns of the wrist and her feet stamped out the rhythm. The dance was meant to be graceful and powerful, but when Naiba tried it, she looked more like she was having some sort of fit.

Cinder scrubbed at the floor all the harder in her panic. "These are the dances of your people. How do you not know them?"

"These aren't our dances any more than those were clannish stone walls," Naiba said bitterly.

Cinder pinched the bridge of her nose between her fingers and thumb. "Let's focus on your singing then—you *can* sing, right?"

Naiba took a deep breath and let out a few crystal-clear notes in Luathan. Cinder looked over the girl again with new eyes. Though she wasn't beautiful, she had an innocent freshness about her. With Storm's and Ash's help with makeup, the girl could probably be made into something near pretty.

"For now, forget the dancing," Cinder told her. "Let's just focus on your singing."

Naiba wrung her hands. "If . . . if I fail, where will she send me?"

To a place where you will be used up like the rags I'm scrubbing the floor with, Cinder thought sadly. By helping with Naiba's training, was Cinder trading this girl's future for her own freedom? She pushed aside her guilt. Not training Naiba would only result in lower bids or the girl being sold off somewhere worse. "There's no point in worrying about that," Cinder said. "Right now, I want you to worry about what Luathan song you should sing."

Naiba closed her eyes and opened her mouth. A somber, haunting rush of sounds broke forth. Cinder could sense the loneliness, even if she couldn't understand the words. They worked on each note—when to hold it and when to let it go. How to build the song from something soft and gentle into a crescendo that left chills on Cinder's arms.

By dinnertime, the great room shone from top to bottom. Cinder hadn't started on the dress yet, but she was beginning to feel a measure of hope that she could pull this off.

That night, she helped the companions serve their men and immediately cleaned up any spills or crumbs. As the evening wore on, Cinder grew increasingly tired. She'd slept so little over the last few months that she was rarely without a headache. She was tempted to try a bite of the lamb chops, but Zura's spies were always watching.

When the last of the companions had retreated to their rooms with the men, Cinder went to the servants' house. In the kitchen, Storm was clearing away the last of the dishes. Cinder took a bowl of lentils and counted each bite as she wound her way up the stairs to the stiflingly hot attic room. Naiba was already asleep. Cinder longed to join her, but she had only one day to finish the dress.

She sat down on her broken stool and gathered the rich fabric into her hands. Afraid of making a mistake in her exhausted state, she measured twice before cutting anything. Still, she cut the last panel too small. She stared hopelessly at the useless piece of fabric. No doubt Zura would make her pay to buy more. And she dared not try to hide it, because Zura always found out.

Cinder pressed her fingers into her burning eyes and rubbed them until they watered. Her thoughts would be clearer in the morning. The night had cooled considerably, as it always did in the desert. Bracing herself for the coming darkness, she blew out the lamp, then pushed to her feet and reached out to close the window. Below, a hooded figure slipping from the mansion made her pause. Instead of heading to the outbuildings, the person, clearly a woman, glanced around carefully. Instinctively, Cinder ducked behind the sill just as the shadowed gaze turned her direction. When Cinder peeked out again, the woman was moving toward the back gate.

Cinder tensed. Didn't the companions all know about the new guard? Where was he, anyway? She searched the wall but couldn't see him. The woman was headed straight for danger. Cinder almost opened her mouth in warning. Before she could, a form detached from beneath one of the garden trees and snatched the woman. Cinder swallowed a gasp.

What would he do to her? Worse yet, what would Zura do? The guard spun the woman around and said something too low for Cinder to make out. And then he laughed. Cinder scrambled to come up with some way to help that didn't make things worse.

But instead of dragging the woman back to the mansion, he wrapped his arms around her and kissed her. Stunned, Cinder gaped at the two as they stumbled toward the garden shed. The guard broke away from the woman just long enough to push open the door. Before the pair disappeared inside the shed, golden lamplight bathed the man's long face, revealing a strange mark on his cheek.

Cinder gripped the windowsill so hard her fingers hurt. A companion risked death by consorting with anyone other than her clients. Disgusted by the woman's carelessness and lack of regard for her own safety, Cinder moved to the washbasin and wetted her finger before dipping it in salt and polishing her teeth—fifteen strokes on each side. She washed her face and shaved the sides of her scalp, then turned to go to bed. Beyond the window, the shed door swinging open caught her gaze. She shot a searing gaze at the two lovers.

The woman was adjusting her clannish dress, but the man grabbed her arm and pulled her back to him. Just before their lips met, her upturned face caught the light.

Cinder's arms fell limply at her sides. It was Ash. Her mother kissed the guard, whose hands were all over her. Then she pulled back and tugged her hood over her head. The man slapped her behind on his way to unlock the gate, and Ash disappeared from view. Cinder's mother would never be that stupid. Would never risk her life and the lives of her daughter and mother to slip outside the House of Night. Not unless she had a very good reason.

Before Cinder knew what she was doing, she had slipped into her own cloak and tugged the hood down low over her face. She grabbed the closest thing she had to a weapon—a pair of scissors—and tucked them deep in the pockets of her robes. Her gaze searched the shadows where her grandmother slept. At least Cinder hoped she was sleeping.

"Where are you going?" a voice suddenly asked.

Cinder's head swiveled toward Naiba's dark form beside her grandmother. "Out to the privy." She felt the girl's eyes on her, felt her hesitation, as if she knew Cinder was lying. There was a rustling sound and a long moment of silence. Naiba must have lain back down.

Relieved, Cinder counted her steps as she stole past the row of women. Soon she slipped into the velvety darkness and rushed toward the shed. She chewed on the inside of her cheek—if her mother was caught, she would be sold. And despite her years in Arcina, Ash did not know the streets. Cinder had to know why she would risk so much.

The guard turned around. When he saw Cinder, he jumped. "Get back in the house!" he snapped, his voice low. "No one is to be near the wall after dark."

"I must follow my mother."

He took a step closer. It was too dark to make out his features other than that he was lanky, with big ears sticking out against the star-strewn sky. When he grinned, his teeth flashed in the moonlight. "Twice in one night, and a new one at that."

Cinder's hand crept to her scissors, the weight of them reassuring in her grip. "I'm in a hurry. I need to get through."

He cocked her a grin, his gaze sliding down her cloaked figure. "Me too."

Before she could react, the guard had her pressed up against the gate, his wet lips plastered against her mouth. She struggled against him, but his grip was like iron. She jerked out her scissors, then grabbed the back of his neck and held the point to his throat. "Give me the keys."

The guard tried to maneuver away from the knife, but Cinder held him in place and pushed the point into the delicate skin. He froze and she felt his throat working—one, two, three times. "And what do you think the mother will do when I tell her you took off?" he gasped.

"What do you think she'll do when she finds out you bedded my mother and tried to bed me? You know we're not for the likes of you."

"As if she'll believe you!"

Cinder gritted her teeth and pushed the scissors far enough that she knew she was drawing blood. She remembered the mark on the man's cheek and suddenly realized what it was: a single-flame tattoo that was given to the queen's redeemed—men who had once been criminals. In Idara's time of need, Nelay had freed them, promising their marks of shame would turn to marks of honor if they proved themselves. But this man's mark had not been finished. He had run, deserting his people in their darkest hour.

"And she would be more likely to believe the word of a fallen?" Cinder hissed. The guard didn't respond. "You're going to let me go. And you're going to let me back in. If you don't say a word, then neither will I about what you did to my mother."

Very slowly, the guard took the key from around his neck and inserted it in the lock. With a snick, it gave way behind Cinder. She scrambled out and slammed it shut. Hopefully Zura or one of her spies hadn't heard the commotion. Cinder held the gate shut for a moment, waiting for the guard to come after her. Instead, the lock snicked again.

Relieved, she whirled toward the empty streets. Her mother was nowhere in sight. Cinder's gaze darted down the three possible routes, not knowing which her mother would have taken. She jumped up to grab the branch of a tree next to the tallest building and started climbing. When she reached the top, her hands were sticky with sap. She stretched out and took hold of a roof beam that stuck out from the mud-brick walls. She hooked her leg around the beam, pulled herself onto the roof, and peered into the night, glad for the light of the moon. She saw nothing to the west or south, but a dark figure moved to the east.

She had no way of knowing if the person was her mother or not, but Cinder didn't have any other options. She took hold of a roof beam and dangled over the street before letting herself drop. She hit hard, her knees jarred and her feet stinging. Ignoring the pain, she sprinted silently through the deserted streets, counting her steps as she went. She carried her scissors firmly in her hand. The city watch was good at their job, but the shadows were deep, and this part of the city seemed eerily silent. Not even a glimmer of lamp light could be seen in the windows.

Cinder could taste blood on the back of her throat 1,958 steps later, when she caught up to the figure and confirmed it was her mother. Ash was hurrying along, the long dagger in her grip a deterrent to anyone who might think to molest her.

Tugging her veil over her face, Cinder hung back and tried to keep her steps silent. She'd counted 3,453 steps when her mother moved to the eastern side of the city, not far from the palace. Here, there were still lights on and people about, most of them drunk or up to no good, or both. Ash stepped toward a tavern called the Sand Snake. Cinder ducked behind an empty street-vendor cart just as her mother looked back. Breathless, Cinder waited to see if she'd been discovered. Seven heartbeats passed before Ash turned away. A moment later, she disappeared inside the tavern.

Frozen with indecision, Cinder watched two people stumble outside, sound and light coming with them. Despite the late hour, closer to morning than evening, the tavern sounded busy. Hoping she could blend in, Cinder checked her veil and hurried after her mother. Tribesmen filled the tavern. Rather than the rich colors Idarans preferred, the tribesmen's robes were a nondescript tan, meant to blend in with the desert. They didn't wear tattoos on their scalps, either. Their accents were fine and sharp, like sand blasting against Cinder's skin.

Her mother sat at a table with one of the tribesmen, an untouched drink before her. Checking to make sure her veil was tightly secured, Cinder kept her eyes down and sat on the cushions at the short table behind her mother. She could hear Ash's voice, low and urgent, but she couldn't make out the words. She was speaking to a thin man in his forties with a piercing gaze.

Out of the corner of her eye, Cinder saw her mother hand the man something wrapped in a bit of cloth. He opened it, smiled, and leaned back in his seat. Cinder stood up, waving at the tavern maid as an excuse to see what the man held—rubies sparkled like crystallized blood. It was an earring Cinder had seen her mother wearing the night before.

She couldn't even begin to guess the value of the items her mother had stolen. Fire and burning, Zura would kill her for it. Under her veil, Cinder pressed her hand to her mouth and tapped her fingers to distract herself from throwing up.

A girl wearing a stained apron came to stand before her. "What would you like?"

"I'm waiting for someone," Cinder said, the words barely above a whisper.

The girl huffed. "Well then, why did you wave me over?"

Cinder muttered some excuse. By the time she had her wits about her, her mother was already slipping out the door and back into the night. Cinder bolted after her, determined to catch up and demand to know what was going on. But Cinder had no sooner left the building than a hand clamped around her mouth, and a strong arm rolled her off her feet and spun her into the alley flanking the tavern.

She struggled, reaching for her scissors, yet his grip—he was too strong to be a woman—only tightened until she saw stars. He pinned her against the wall and searched her. He found her scissors and took them. "Who are you?" His voice was gruff and hard.

"I don't have any money," Cinder gasped. "Just scissors, and you already have them." *By the Balance, please don't let him want anything else.* She had managed to fend off the guard, but this man was obviously better trained and unbelievably strong. She didn't stand a chance at stopping him if he wanted to molest her.

He pushed his forearm against her throat, and she struggled to breath. "Why were you following the woman? Why did you eavesdrop on their conversation?"

Cinder didn't see any point in lying. "Because I had to know."

"Know what?"

"Why she would do something so stupid!" she wheezed.

The man had just drawn breath to ask another question when someone else hurried into the alley and reported, "No one else was following Ash."

The man holding Cinder wrenched her around and tied her hands behind her with quick, efficient movements. Then he forced her toward the rear of the tavern, to a set of stairs leading below ground. She struggled all the harder, remembering all the times Zura had locked her in the cellar for the slightest disobedience. The other man grabbed Cinder's legs, and they hauled her into a lamp-lit room, where they pushed her into a chair.

Her gaze darted around the room. She needed one window—just one. But there were only four cloistered walls, covered by city maps with markings she couldn't read. She closed her eyes, and rocked, counting.

"You?" a voice said in surprise.

Cinder forced her eyes open. Standing before her was Darsam, the lord's son who'd nearly killed her with a chariot. She tried to glare at him but was afraid it came off as begging. "What do you want with me?"

His eyes widened in surprise. "You followed a woman from the House of Night into the tavern. Eavesdropped on her conversation. I want to know who you're working for. Did Zura send you? Jatar?"

Trying to keep up with his questions, Cinder shook her head. "Send me?"

Darsam loomed over her, his hands bracing the table on either side of her. "Girls go missing in the city all the time. The streets aren't safe at night." Fear churned in Cinder's belly. "Now, tell me who you're working for and—"

Two beads of sweat raced down each side of her temple. "I'm not working for anyone! Ash is my mother! I saw her sneaking out and followed her."

Darsam stared at Cinder then, his eyes widening with understanding. She had never been this grateful to look so much like her mother.

"If that's true, why are you acting so guilty? And why did you follow her?" Darsam asked in a softer voice.

One, two, three, four hot tears of fear and exhaustion and anger rushed down Cinder's cheek. She hated them—wished she could make them stop, but they only came faster. *Five, six, seven, eight.* "Zura punished us by locking us in the cellar. For days, sometimes. I can't—" Panic welled up again, stronger than even before. "I don't do well underground. I followed my mother to find out why she would risk her life . . . had to make sure she was all right. She doesn't know the streets like I do. It's dangerous out here."

The guard at the door took a step closer and said to Darsam, "What do you want us to do with her?"

Darsam gazed thoughtfully at Cinder, then straightened and removed her scissors from his pocket. When she stiffened, he held out a placating hand. "I'm just going to cut you free."

Not completely trusting him, she leaned forward. Three seconds later, her hands came free. She rubbed out the stinging in her wrists, wiped the tears from her face with her sleeves, and pushed to her feet. "Why did my mother come here?"

Darsam handed the scissors to her and watched as she pushed them into the pocket of her robes. "Ask her that for yourself, Cinder."

Surprised he remembered her name, she asked, "What do you have to do with it?"

He didn't answer. Grunting, Cinder edged around him and headed for the door. The man standing before it shot a questioning glace at Darsam, who must have given some sign that she could go, for the guard stepped aside and let her rush out into the dark night. She pounded up five steps before she stumbled and fell, bruising her knee.

A hand behind her pulled her to her feet. "I'll see you there safely."

Cinder resisted the urge to pull out of Darsam's grip. "I would prefer to get there on my own." He didn't respond but simply walked beside her, his pace matching hers. "Why won't you tell me what's going on?" she asked him.

"That's your mother's secret to tell."

"I saw the earring she gave to the man she met with. When Zura finds out it's missing, there will be beatings. And someone will be sold. Even killed."

After a long pause, Darsam said, "I mean you and your family no harm, Cinder."

"You've already done us harm," she replied through clenched teeth. She had to think of a way out of this. Some way to stop the events already set in motion. "Give the earring back to me. I'll make it look like it was merely dropped. Ash will be caned for losing it, but—"

"It's too late for that now."

Cinder glanced up at the lightening sky and picked up her pace. "Too late for the spoiled son of the city lord to care about some lowly prostitutes?" When Darsam didn't answer, she felt a moment of fear at the memory of his unforgiving grip.

"If you are free, as you say, why must you go back?" he asked.

"I'm 160 attalics in debt."

"And if you leave, your mother and grandmother would suffer for it," he surmised tightly. "Why were you counting, back in the basement?"

A flush of shame worked its way up from Cinder's neck. "It helps calm me." Now she could see the rear gate to the House of Night.

"Do you have a way back in?" he asked.

"I hope so." She took the last thirty-three steps, then paused at the ornate door and rapped lightly. There was no answer, no snicking of the lock.

Heart pounding, she said as loudly as she dared, "Let me in."

"See, there was your mistake," said the guard's voice. "Zura would have known that I let Ash go. But she's back now. And you aren't—you, the girl with a history of sneaking out."

Cinder slapped the flat of her hand against the door. "And you who let me escape!"

"You should have let me have my fun. Then you wouldn't be in this position. Of course, I *am* the forgiving sort."

She swore at him, promising more than one kind of violence. The guard chuckled lightly and his feet scuffed as he moved away.

"Is there another way in?" Darsam asked.

Cinder rested her forehead on the gate. "I doubt he'll let me pick the lock and slip back inside."

"You can pick a lock?"

She patted her breast wrap. "I never go anywhere without my tension wrench and rake pin."

She turned to find him watching her with something like admiration in his gaze. He headed north. "Come on."

After a moment's hesitation, she followed him and said, "Why?" He didn't answer. She rolled her eyes. "I'm sure this is all terribly exciting for a man for whom the consequences don't apply, but I need to find a rope. So unless you're heading to one . . ."

Darsam looked back and forth as if searching for something. Now it was light enough that she could make out his well-muscled body and the features of his face. He was breathtakingly handsome.

He found an abandoned cart and took hold of the edge. "There's no way you can move that without a couple donkeys or an ox," Cinder commented.

He dug his shoulder in, straining, and the cart inched toward the wall. Her mouth fell open. She'd seen a pair of donkeys struggle to move a cart smaller than this one. A beat later, she settled in beside Darsam, pushing for all she was worth. Once the cart was lined up against the wall, he climbed to the top and held a hand out for her.

Cinder considered not taking it—it had always been hard for her to touch men—but he had helped her without any obligation. She let him pull her up and was surprised to find thick calluses on the hands of such a rake. Darsam squatted down and braced himself against the wall. "Straddle my shoulders," he said quietly.

Tapping her fingers in indecision, she looked at his broad back, then up at the slate-gray sky. There wasn't time for another option. Cinder sat on his shoulders and he rose smoothly. "Now, stand on my shoulders and haul yourself up," he told her.

She'd seen street performers do this before. Darsam held his hands up for her. She placed her sweaty palms against his dry ones and rose to her feet. Wobbling a little, she had to stand on her tiptoes to reach the top of the wall, but she didn't have the arm strength to haul herself up the rest of the way. Without hesitation, he stepped up onto the raised edge of the cart and rose onto his tiptoes, boosting Cinder just high enough to hook her hands on the other side of the brick. She took hold of the wall and scrambled up. Straddling it, she looked down at him.

He shot her a grin and hopped off the cart.

"Were you a street performer at one point?" she said quietly.

"No, but I know a few." He dug his shoulder into the cart and started pushing it back into place.

Cinder was reluctant to leave without answers to her questions, but she could already smell the smoke from Storm's cooking fire. She swung her other foot over the wall and dropped to the ground.

CHAPTER FIVE

Cinder paused at the door to the kitchen. Her grandmother was already at the long table, muttering to herself as the knife skinned mangos. Cinder didn't see any of the other girls about. She swallowed hard, her fingers tapping frantically against her thigh, and stepped inside the room.

"Where have you been?" her grandmother demanded.

Cinder hesitated, reluctant to admit she had followed Ash when she didn't even know what her mother was doing yet. "I went to one more place to see about a job."

Her grandmother pursed her lips. "You should be working on getting Naiba ready. Her auction is tonight!"

Cinder nodded. "I'm almost finished with the dress."

"I got up early this morning and worked on it a little for you," Storm informed her. "If you take it to your mother, she can stay up today while you do your chores."

Cinder's eyes filled with tears. "Thank you."

Her grandmother smiled. "Now, hurry up and rouse the others. I've let them sleep too long because I was waiting for you."

Cinder sent the other servants downstairs so she could finish the hems. Naiba lingered by the window, staring out over the city. "Last night, where did you go?"

"The privy," Cinder answered.

"With your cloak and scissors?"

Cinder tried to keep the shock off her face. "You must have been mistaken."

"When you didn't come back," Naiba went on, "I sat by the window, waiting. I saw Ash come back through the gate. I saw the guard . . . touching her. Zura came into the back gardens. She would have seen them. I managed to distract her long enough for your mother to get away."

Cinder gaped at her. "You did what?"

Naiba shrugged off the shoulder of her robe, revealing fresh welts.

"Why—why would you help us?" Cinder asked. She didn't think any of the other servants would risk so much, and they'd known each other their entire lives.

"Because your mother would have suffered a lot more than just a beating." Naiba pulled up her robe. "I don't know what you two are doing, but I've seen slaves killed for less."

Cinder winced. All this time, she'd thought of this girl as an irritating child. But there was steel beneath the surface. "Thank you, Naiba."

The girl's hands curled into fists. "Yula. My name is Yula."

Cinder placed her hand over her heart. "You have to keep your true name in here, where they can never take it from you." She wouldn't even dare think of the girl as Yula, in case it slipped out.

Naiba bowed her head. "I wanted someone to know." She turned and headed downstairs after the others.

Cinder stared at her retreating form. Naiba had saved her mother's life, and possibly Cinder's as well. She swore that from now on, she would do everything in her power to make sure Naiba survived this.

When it was time to take the food into the mansion, Cinder was so tired she wasn't sure how she would finish all her cleaning and the dress. Her eyes felt gritty and her head heavy as she carried the trays to the rooms. Before she pushed into her mother's room, she paused to collect herself.

As always, Ash was sitting at the table, her lip stain faded and cracked from her escapades the night before. Unable to meet her gaze, Cinder lifted the tea pot and asked, "Do you believe I'm good enough to become the seamstress for the House of Night?"

Her mother looked up in surprise. "Yes."

As Cinder poured the tea, she said softly, "Then why did you risk everything I'm working for to visit the Sand Snake?"

Ash's hand shot out, gripping Cinder's arm hard enough to leave a mark. The teapot slipped from her grasp and shattered on the tiles. Hot water sprayed on Cinder's legs and soaked the bottoms of her sandaled feet. Hissing in pain, she jumped back. Ash dropped to her knees and soaked up the liquid with a tea towel before it could escape along the six grout lines. She didn't shy away from the heat as she brushed the fragments into the center.

"You followed me." Ash's lips barely betrayed the words.

Cinder tried to stop her brain from calculating the cost of the china. "I saw you with the guard at the gate," she whispered, the tears she refused to shed making her head throb. "And I wasn't the only one."

"Who?"

"She won't tell anyone."

"You're sure?"

Cinder nodded.

Ash's eyes slipped closed. "It isn't anything I haven't done before—a thousand times before. What's once more, especially when that once more serves me instead of her?" Still on her knees, she looked up at Cinder. "You have to trust me."

"Not until you tell me why."

"The walls," Ash pleaded.

"They can't hear us."

"They don't have to hear us."

Cinder knelt on the floor, which still felt hot from the water. "You have to get the earring back," she whispered. "When Zura finds it missing, she'll come after you." Her mother didn't answer. "Do you know what you're risking?"

Ash leaned forward. "I have survived as a slave longer than you have been alive—and I did it because I understand people in a way you never will. Now, you will keep silent. Do you understand?"

Cinder felt the heat swelling up to her head. "I'm going to be a seamstress in a few days. Then I can buy all of your freedom. You just have to trust me."

Ash laughed, but there was no humor in it. "There are pockets of darkness and cruelty in the world, Daughter. And Zura revels in those shadows. Do not mistake her kindness for anything other than the mask it is."

The main door swung open. There stood Magian, watching Cinder and Ash with narrowed eyes. "What's going on here?" she barked.

"I knocked over the teapot," Ash said immediately.

Did Magian know they had snuck out last night? Cinder gathered six fragments into her hand and transferred them onto the tray without looking up.

"Whispering is not allowed in the House," Magian said.

"We don't want to wake my patron," Ash replied.

Magian huffed. "Ash, you will come to my rooms for your five lashes after your patron leaves."

Ash inclined her head in submission. Cinder let out a breath—Magian and Zura didn't know about last night. "Cinder, the broken pot will come out of your wages," Magian went on. "This whispering stops or Ash will be sent to live with Rugur for a time. He's been requesting it."

Rugur was a big man with a mean streak. Ash's hands closed into fists. "It won't happen again, Magian."

"Cinder, this arrived for you." Magian nodded to a small wooden chest on the floor by her feet. She must have set it there before knocking.

Eyes downcast, Cinder took the chest and opened it. Inside were hundreds of glass jewels, all of them faceted. Fighting the urge to sort and count them, she closed the lid. She could do this. She could save herself and her family. If she could just manage to keep her mother from dooming them first.

Magian started away. After casting a pleading look at her mother, Cinder hurried to catch up with Zura's daughter and asked, "Might I work on the dress today?"

"You went without sleep for months while searching for a job and sewing your own clothing. You can go without sleep now."

Gradually, Cinder became aware of a low murmur of conversation. It suddenly occurred to her that she was asleep, and that the auction was tonight and the dress still wasn't ready. She bolted up in her chair to find the dress on the form, the glass already sewn onto the fabric. In the muted evening light, it glittered like light sparking off the tops of waves. Cinder glanced around the room to see Ash sitting beside Naiba on the bench, containers of colored powders and brushes littering the makeup dresser beside her. Cinder's mother leaned forward, her expert hands applying the powders to the girl's face.

"The dress is done?" Cinder asked.

"We finished it while you slept," Ash said without taking her eyes from her work.

"You fell asleep with the needle in your hands," Naiba added.

Feeling a rush of affection for the girl, Cinder walked to the dress and lifted one of the panels. She was shocked at how beautiful and unique it was—even more so than the other robes she had made.

"There." Ash tossed the brushes back onto the table. "What do you think?"

Cinder looked up, her vision stained crimson from the dress. A light powder dusted Naiba's face. Kohl lined her eyes, and a pale pink stained her mouth. She looked like a scared little girl. Cinder's heart nearly broke as she thought of everything that had been taken from Naiba. Everything that would continue to be taken from her. "She looks lovely," Cinder said softly.

Naiba drew her knees into her chest and hugged them. "What will it be like?"

Ash rested her hands on the girl's. "There will be music and fine food—the best you've ever tasted, and unlike me, you're skinny enough that Zura will let you have all you want. You will serve the men and then sing for them."

"I can't," Naiba squeaked. "I can't talk to them. I can't sing in front of them, knowing what they mean to do to me."

Cinder came to kneel beside her. "I promise you, all you have to do is sing for them. You're too young for the rest."

Ash shot Cinder a disapproving look she didn't understand.

Naiba dropped her head. "What if I fail?"

If Naiba failed, Cinder would never be truly free. But for Naiba, it would be far worse. "You won't."

The door swept open, startling all four of them. Farush stepped into the room, followed by his brother, who bore a large chest. Zura and Magian entered last. Zura's eyes swept over Naiba, and a small smile pulled at the corners of her lips. "Are you ready to prove that you belong in the House of Night and not in some back alley?" demanded the mistress.

Naiba dropped her head. "Yes, Mother."

Zura circled the girl while Magian sifted through the chest Farood had set next to the bed. Magian laid out the jewelry for the night, marking everything on her scrolls. Cinder wondered how long before they noticed an earring was missing.

Having finished her circuit of Naiba, Zura paused before Cinder and gestured to Magian. When her daughter didn't see her, Zura snapped her fingers. Magian removed a few trays of jewelry and pulled out one of the robes Cinder had made—this one in deepest purple. It had been her mother's robe long ago. Cinder remembered gathering fistfuls of the gauzy fabric in her fevering hands as her mother had held her.

"Put it on," Zura said to Naiba.

"But Mother, I specifically made the red dress to display my skills," Cinder protested.

Zura's gaze swung to her. "Who better to show off the design than yourself?"

"You want me to wear it?" Cinder's mouth came open. "But . . . I made it for Naiba."

Zura waved away her words with a lazy flick of her wrist. "The color is all wrong and the texture too heavy for her. You should have waited until you met the girl before picking the fabric. You always sew lacing into the back, so it should fit you. Perhaps a little tight, but the men won't mind."

Cinder counted six heartbeats and one ragged inhale and exhale. "You want me to attend the auction?"

Zura turned on her heel. "Do her hair and makeup, Ash," she ordered before signaling Magian and the thugs to follow her from the room.

Once the door was shut, Cinder shot a helpless look at her mother, but Ash said quietly, "The walls are always listening."

Somehow, Cinder knew they were listening now. In a daze, she sat on the chair and felt the tickle of the makeup brushes, smelled the powders on her own skin. Ash piled Cinder's hair on her head to show off the freeborn tattoos. Cinder dropped her plain, worn robes to the floor. She pulled the dress off the form and slipped it over her head, marveling at how heavy it was. Still, the material was soft, the gown surprisingly comfortable. Her mother tightened the corset laces on the back until the bodice fit snugly across Cinder's breasts.

Cinder bowed down under the weight of the gown and tied on the two gold sandals encrusted with bits of clear, faceted glass. Magian had left her some jewelry too—ruby-and-gold anklets and a beautifully worked belt that was a mockery of the clannish belts.

Cinder straightened, then looked at herself in the mirror. What she saw took her breath away. The dark kohl made her silver eyes smolder. Her hair was intricately braided in the manner of the clanswomen. She looked like her mother and grandmother, only the crimson dress emphasized her curves more than any robe or overdress ever could. The glass Cinder had stitched with such care caught the light with each movement of her body, making even the slightest shift look like a dazzling display.

Ash eyed her sadly. "Would that you were an ugly child."

Cinder wrung her hands. "Zura is letting me show off my designs, probably to see how the patrons react."

Her mother turned and strode to the door, then paused with her back to Cinder and Naiba. "Approach any man not already linked with a companion," she instructed. "Feed them, converse with them, dance with them. Try to be charming. But do not let them lead you to a private room. That is only for patrons and with Zura's approval."

Cinder and Naiba trailed after Ash. Once they left the clanswoman sector, Cinder could smell the food and hear the music. Ash, Naiba, and Cinder stepped into the lamplight. The mansion's great room already teemed with men. Companions mingled, bringing their patrons wines and dainty treats. Some of the men had gathered around low tables surrounded by velvet cushions. Others had sidled up to their companions or pulled them into private sitting rooms. Some couples were dancing.

A man perhaps in his late twenties came straight to Ash and pressed a passionate kiss to her mouth. Cinder turned away, hot with embarrassment, and tapped her fingers to her thumb.

"I've missed you, my clanwoman," the man said.

Her name is Ash, Cinder thought darkly.

Ash smiled up at him. "And I you. How is your business? Are the tribesmen still raiding your caravans?"

He made a sound low in his throat. "Terribly. Blasted smugglers have stolen nearly half of my dried mangos!" Then he noticed Cinder and asked in a stunned voice, "Is she your daughter?"

Ash started pulling him away. "Come along, Kaveh. There is wine on the tables."

He resisted. "It's remarkable—she looks so like you! Has she had her auction yet?"

Cinder squared herself in front of him. "I am not a companion. I am freeborn. I am here to train the House of Night's newest companion." Cinder started to gesture to Naiba, but found her hiding behind one of the columns. She gave the girl a desperate look and motioned her toward them, taking hold of her arm so she couldn't try to escape. "Naiba is our newest companion. She has a beautiful voice, as you will see later."

Kaveh looked the girl over but was clearly unimpressed. "Well, on to the wine then." He followed Ash, who was all sugary smiles. Yet Cinder could read the lines of fury in her stiff movements.

Trying not to squirm under the intense gazes of the dozens of men, Cinder locked her arm around Naiba's. "Smile at them," she whispered. The girl managed a terrified smile. Cinder let out a long sigh. She needed more sleep. But she might survive the night if she could taste some of the food. "Come on, let's get you something to eat."

She pulled Naiba toward the banquet tables, which were crowded with every kind of food imaginable, divided into sections from each nation. There was whale soup from the highmen, leopard skewers from Luatha, and even a stew of vegetables and lamb from the clanlands. Unable to resist, Cinder filled a plate and nearly fainted at the smoky taste of the meat. Naiba was just as bad, drinking a bowl of soup without pause.

A voice came from over the girls' shoulders. "Take the food to the men. It's a good way to break the ice."

Inundated by the scent of her mother's jasmine perfume, Cinder swallowed. "Which ones?"

"Choose the men with the kindest eyes and the richest clothes," her mother replied, then loaded a plate with food and hurried back to Kaveh's side.

Cinder took a bowl of soup, Naiba a plate of skewers. Counting the men who watched them like a hawk watching a duckling, she noticed many of their eyes settling on her. She took a deep breath and steered Naiba away from the men who stared at the young girl with a sick kind of fascination. "The more you impress them, the more money you'll bring and the better you'll be endowed," Cinder told her.

Naiba squared herself and glanced around the room. With Cinder trailing her, the girl walked over to an older man with a bushy beard and dark eyes. Naiba placed the bowl in his hands and did a little bow before turning away.

Cinder grabbed the girl's arm and pulled her back to the man. "This is Naiba. She's to be our newest companion. She's brilliant with Luathan songs."

The man stroked his beard one, two, three times. "I have a meeting coming up with a possible buyer from the Adrack. If she's as good as you say, well, her youth might leave him a touch softened for the deal."

Cinder gave him a bright smile.

He looked over Naiba again. "Of course, it would also be nice to hear of the rustic ways of the Luathan—and you know how tribesmen are with their stories. Does she know any?"

Cinder turned an expectant gaze toward Naiba, who was staring at the man's chest. Cinder squeezed her arm, and Naiba said, "I used to tell stories to my sisters. Stories of the three virgin goddesses and their three horses—thunder, lightning, and wind."

The man rubbed his hands together. "Excellent. Most promising."

Cinder gave a little bow and began steering Naiba away. "If you will please excuse us." When they were out of earshot of the man, Cinder said, "Now was that so bad?"

Naiba gave a small shake of her head. "No. Not bad at all."

Cinder was giddy with hope. "We're going to pull this off. You will wear the finest clothes and eat the finest foods and travel the city telling stories and singing songs."

Naiba smiled weakly and gathered up another plate of food. Cinder scanned the room, searching for another kind-looking man with an honest expression. A portly man with a piggish nose and red skin caught her eye. There was a sort of jolliness about him—he was the type of man who liked his wine and laughter. He lifted his glass to Cinder and Naiba and made a little bow.

"There." Cinder pointed. "Why don't you try this one yourself?"

Naiba blanched. "But I don't know what to say!"

Cinder took a deep breath, tapping her fingers and trying to remain patient. "Be kind, Naiba. It's who you are. And maybe he came here looking for a little kindness."

Naiba bit her lip and stepped toward the man. Cinder watched as the girl asked him a hesitant question. He clapped his hand on her shoulder and laughed uproariously. She rewarded him with a timid smile.

At that moment, Cinder noticed Zura tracking Naiba. Her eyes never leaving the other girl's progress, the mistress came to stand beside Cinder and said, "You will circulate food to the men as well."

Cinder's mouth fell open and she forced it shut. "I thought only the companions were allowed to interact—"

"I already told you, more men came tonight than I expected, all of them potential clients. Two men in particular with more money than all the others combined—they're both on the north side. I want them to return. So you will mingle. You will feed them. And you will shine like my companions. Am I clear?"

Cinder barely managed to hold back her anger. "Yes, Mother."

The woman slipped away. Cinder went to the table and filled a plate. In three steps, she had brought it to the first man she saw—an older gentleman with a dizzying amount of tattoos on his head. "You look hungry," she said with a smile.

"And cold," he responded. "I wouldn't mind having you under me to keep me warm."

An image of the man on top of her flashed in her mind. *I'm trapped, I'm trapped, I'm trapped!* Reeling, she returned to the table and steadied herself against it. *I'm not supposed to seduce the men, simply serve them,* she reminded herself. She brought each of them a plate of food with a little bow, not bothering to say a word anymore. To and from the table she counted her steps, making sure she always landed on an even number.

A little shriek of dismay broke her counting, and the numbers fell to pieces all around her. She whirled around. One of the men had pulled Naiba into his lap. Cinder shoved a plate of food into a man's unsuspecting hands. "Farush! Farood!" she called.

Seven steps later, she hauled a cowering Naiba out of the man's grasp. "Show some respect. She's training to be a companion, not a common whore. And she's only twelve years old!"

The man jumped to his feet and stood far too close to Cinder. "That's not what I heard."

Cinder fisted her hands on her hips. "Well, you've heard wrong."

Zura was suddenly there, her thugs beside her. "Problem, sir?"

He turned a glare onto her. "I was told—"

She held up a hand to silence him. "Perhaps you are new to companion houses, but there is no touching of the companions—in training or otherwise—by anyone other than their assigned patrons. Granted, many men succumb to the temptation on their first visits. Perhaps a distraction is in order. Would you like to come with me to one of the private rooms? I have some Luathan berry wine I'd like you to sample. Or perhaps you're more of a spirits man? I have some fine rye whiskey all the way from the clanlands." Zura expertly steered the man away.

Cinder turned to a cowering Naiba, who folded her arms across herself. "Are those the kind of men who will be my patrons?" the girl asked, her bottom lip quivering.

Cinder reached out with a shaking hand and tucked a stray strand of hair behind Naiba's ear. "I promise you won't have to worry about any men like that. The House of Night is the finest and most respected companion house in the city."

Naiba approached five more men, with Cinder by her side. Twice she had to steer the girl away when the conversation turned lewd after only a few words. How had the sods even been let inside? Cinder gestured to Farush and Farood, who came over to take the men to the tasting room with Zura. After two more, Naiba had just started to gain a little confidence, so Cinder let her try on her own again, staying close the whole time.

Most of the men at the gathering appeared to be over forty years old, but now Cinder and Naiba approached a cluster of young men. In the center, his eyes never leaving Cinder's face, was Darsam. Laughing loudly at a joke, he seemed much different than the quiet, steady man she'd encountered last night. Instead of dark, plain robes and swords, he wore fine linen with an embroidered vest that spoke of money. His face was shaved after the manner of the tribesmen.

Tapping her fingers to her thigh, Cinder felt a flush of shame. He would never believe she was not a companion now that he had seen her serving. Reminding herself that it didn't matter what Darsam thought, she turned to look for Naiba, only to find her headed toward them. When the girl offered him a bowl of soup, Darsam laughed and waved her off. Naiba's eyes fell and she hurried away.

Ten fingers curling into a fist, Cinder stormed over to him. "What are you doing here?"

"Can't you guess?" he teased.

She had thought him different from the rest. A spoiled man playing at criminal, yes, but maybe a decent criminal. Apparently, that was only a front. So he was just like every other man she knew. Anger tingled along Cinder's scalp, lifting her hair. "Why did you humiliate her?"

Darsam cocked an eyebrow. "Who?"

Cinder took a breath to compose herself. "Naiba. Her auction is tonight. Would it have hurt you to take the soup?"

He tugged the plate from Cinder's reluctant hands, then picked up a skewer and took a bite. "I wanted to talk to you, not her."

Cinder narrowed her eyes. Despite his careless manner, there was something different about this man and the others with him. Some kind of quiet readiness instead of insatiable hunger. Were they here about the earring Ash had given to Darsam's cohort? About whatever deal Cinder's mother had made with them? Cinder studied this man and then said softly, "Give it back. Before it costs her something she can't afford to lose."

Darsam held her gaze. "If she isn't willing to risk the price, neither are we."

Cinder opened her mouth to ask what that meant when he caught her arm, his fingers gentle but firm. "I must speak with you privately," he whispered. The flippant manner was gone again, the serious man back, like he'd slipped off a mask. She wondered which mask was really Darsam, or if neither of them was.

She turned and saw Naiba speaking with another man. "I can't leave her."

Darsam looked at Cinder expectantly. "There's not a lot you can do for her. There never was."

"What?" she gasped.

He extended a hand. "Please come with me."

Not certain she should trust him, Cinder almost didn't follow. But he hadn't grabbed her or demanded; he had said please. As if she had a choice. Worry over her mother cinched her resolve, and she trailed after him into the soft shadows of the colonnade that led to the kitchens. The hot air throbbed against her skin. The monsoon would start any moment.

Darsam glanced back at the kitchen, where a couple of lanterns highlighted his face, then at the shadows as if to make sure he and Cinder were truly alone. He looked at her and said softly,

"You have a good heart and an innocence about you. I never would have expected that. But you need to trust your mother and no one else."

"Including you?"

"You would be a fool to. But I am helping you."

Cinder stepped back, unnerved by his nearness. "Help me? Can you free me from the prison? Will you pay my debts?"

His brow furrowed. "Prison?"

He must not know about that part. "I made a deal with Zura. If I could make the next girl into a companion worthy of the House, I would be the next seamstress. If not, I go to the debtors' mines." Despite the heat pricking her skin, Cinder shivered.

"Is that what Zura told you?" Darsam asked in disbelief.

Cinder squared herself in front of him. "What kind of deal did you make with my mother? It was to help me escape the mine, wasn't it? They'll kill her for it, you know. Kill her for taking that earring. I won't trade two years in the mines for my mother's life. So you may as well give it back now."

Cinder could feel him staring at her, though it was too dark to see his expression. Suddenly, the heavens opened, the rain coming down in sheets. Despite the protection of the colonnade, she could feel the spray against her skin. "I will face this alone," she said loudly enough to be heard over the storm.

Darsam leaned in, so close her skin prickled with his nearness. "You've never had a chance, Cinder. Not from the start."

The trembling started deep inside her, working its way out of her body until she was shivering. She wrapped her arms around herself to keep from coming apart from the inside out. "What do you mean?"

He gently laid a hand on her arm. "I told you I would help you."

She felt the weight of his fingers, felt his closeness. And the way he was looking at her—almost like he admired her. Then his

74

gaze strayed to her mouth. Heat prickled in her lower belly, and she found herself wanting to be closer, to touch his skin.

With a start, she realized the faint music from the other room had stopped altogether. She'd left Naiba alone for far too long. She backpedaled. "I must go." She turned and ran for the mansion.

"Cinder!" Darsam called after her. She heard him following. She pushed open one of the pivot doors and slipped inside the building. The dress was damp, and she knew the fabric clung to her and revealed every curve and angle. Her head swung back and forth as she searched the room.

She felt Darsam behind her. "Cinder, please, you need to understand what's happening."

Suddenly, the man whom her mother had met with at the Sand Snake was beside him, pulling him back. "You're attracting too much attention."

Darsam's jaw tightened stubbornly. "Ashar, she doesn't know."

Ashar gripped his arm. "Move, Sam." The older man practically dragged Darsam away from Cinder.

She scanned the crowd and saw Naiba standing with Zura on the platform. Holding an intricately carved box, the mistress smiled and said, "We are pleased to announce that thirty-four new patrons have been added to the House of Night."

Thirty-four? Cinder would have been shocked to hear of more than ten. In a daze, she wove through the crowd toward the platform.

"Magian and I will bring your contracts in the next few days. We are so very pleased to add you to Naiba's roster." Magian handed out peaches to Naiba's new patrons. There was the pig-faced man, grinning and holding the peach like a prize. Then the man who had pulled Naiba into his lap. The man who'd shown interest in the girl's stories. And then the three men who'd made obscene comments.

Zura had accepted all of them.

"There has to be some kind of mistake," Cinder mouthed, not believing what she was seeing.

Naiba was visibly trembling, her face ashen as Zura led her through the crowd, box in hand, toward someone in front of Cinder—the highest bidder. Cinder forced her way past the pig-faced man and saw the man they were heading toward. Durux. Naiba realized it at the same time and balked, her head shaking frantically.

Before Cinder knew what she was doing, she had rushed over and inserted herself between Zura and Durux, one hand raised to the older woman. "You can't do this."

Instead of slapping her or calling for her guards, Zura lifted a single eyebrow and spoke loudly. "My dearest new patrons, take a moment to meet Naiba." After motioning for her guards to stay behind, Zura took hold of Cinder's arm and led her toward her office. "Naiba earned enough to become a companion— Durux paid very highly for her debut—and you, my dear Cinder, will become a seamstress. Isn't that what you wanted?"

"The House of Night specializes in performers. Naiba is twelve years old!" Cinder seethed. "That's what I was preparing her for. She's too young to be a prostitute!"

Inside the office, Magian was already hard at work. She barely looked up at Zura and Cinder before continuing to write out contracts. Zura shut the door and moved to slowly pace before her table. "Things are changing—Idara is changing," she told Cinder. "If my house is to survive, so must we."

"Do you know what that monster will do to her?"

"All thanks to *you*. You managed to train her, dress her in these beautiful garments. Everyone is talking about them, by the way. You already have orders." Zura tapped her own index finger. "You've done it. Proven yourself worthy to become my seamstress and trainer for all future girls who come into my house." She paused and smiled cruelly. "From slave's daughter to slave driver—who would have thought you would so easily turn on your own?"

Zura stepped past her and opened the door, giving Cinder a full view of Durux—his big ears pink with excitement and his close-set gaze fixated on Naiba in a way that made Cinder shudder.

"Now, I don't want to hear another word about it. This is a day to celebrate." Zura started out, but Cinder reached out and grabbed her forearm.

"Naiba won't survive him."

Zura lifted her eyebrows at Cinder's hand on her arm. But she didn't slap her and jerk away like Cinder expected. She simply shrugged. "There is a very strict loss-of-life clause in the contract. I will be more than compensated for any damage or death."

Over the older woman's shoulder, Cinder shot Naiba a desperate glance, but the girl was trapped in Durux's gaze. He moved to pry the box from the girl's clenched fists, not bothering to open it. Then he reached out and caught one of the tears streaming down Naiba's cheek and brought it to his lips to taste it.

"She's just a child," Cinder tried again. "You can't hand her over to a monster like Durux!"

Zura produced a sly smile. "There is another way."

Cinder studied her with a growing wariness.

"I've always wanted you as one of my companions, Cinder," Zura went on.

Cinder remembered being sick with a fever one night as a young girl. She'd wanted her mother, not Holla. So, in the dead of night, she had snuck away to her mother's room. There, Cinder had seen for herself what went on between the companions and the patrons. The thought of strange men touching her, possessing her, made her sick. That's how she felt now. Sick and fevered and desperate. "I will *never* be a companion," she told the mistress.

Zura raised a single eyebrow. "Even if I allow you to purchase Naiba to sweeten the deal?" she asked in a low tone. "In fact, I've been holding an auction for you tonight, as well as for Naiba. Because you are a freewoman, we would split your commission 70/30. Within your first year, you could pay off your purchase of Naiba outright. Return her to her poor father. You already have enough potential clients to pay your debts and purchase your whole family in just a few short years."

Cinder had watched the light die from the new companions' eyes. Watched them cover their hard, broken edges with masks of makeup and fine robes. She'd watched her grandmother and mother be caned for failing to please their clients. "I can't," she choked out.

"All because you detest the idea of men touching you?" Zura scoffed. "Because that will happen one day anyway. Might as well be paid for it."

"You did this on purpose," Cinder exclaimed. "Chose a young girl, fully planning to auction her off as a prostitute. Hoping I'd want to help her."

Zura snorted. "I've done much more than that. I spread the word far and wide that I had two possible companions up for auction tonight. The one with the highest bid would become a companion. It was a marketing tactic. I had to do something to save my business from Jatar. And it worked even better than I expected. Do you want to guess which girl had the higher bids?"

"That's why you had me circulating food to the men. Why you had me wear this dress." Dazed, Cinder looked around. She had wondered where her mother was, but now she realized Zura had made sure she was occupied somewhere else and unable to intervene.

Cinder had to choose between saving herself and saving Naiba. But hadn't she already sworn she would do whatever it took to protect the girl? Her eyes slipped closed and when she opened them again, her gaze locked with Darsam's. His expression was hard, fury sparking in his eyes, and she realized he'd known this would happen. Had tried to warn her. He nodded to her once. She blinked in surprise, remembering how he'd asked her to trust him. She counted to ten and then back down again before she turned to Zura.

"There are other ways to make you comply, Cinder," the older woman said. "I don't want to have to use them, but I will."

Cinder's mother, her grandmother. Darsam had been right—Cinder had never had a choice. "I would have a freewoman's terms, which means I have a choice in my patrons?"

Zura nodded. "Within reason."

Cinder felt everything slipping away. Her bright future. Her chance to finally make it in this world. Magian brought out a rolled scroll and held her a quill with a flourish. "I cannot read it," Cinder said, her cheeks burning with humiliation.

Then Darsam was in the office with them, taking the vellum gently from her fingers. His eyes scanned it, his jaw growing harder with each word. Finally, he nodded to Cinder. "It's a fair contract."

She stared into his dark eyes and willed him to give her some sort of hope. He managed a crooked, pained smile, his eyes begging her to trust him. "I'm just trying to help you."

Not the first time he'd said that—and yet, some part of her actually believed him this time. She took a deep breath, let it out, and made her mark on the line.

Zura rolled up the parchment with a flourish and strode toward the platform. She held both her hands in the air, calling for quiet. When the room finally went still, she proclaimed, "And the winning companion for the night is Cinder!"

With those words, Cinder's knees buckled. She knelt on the floor, bracing herself with her hand to keep from falling over. Her eyes shut against the dizziness assaulting her. *I can't breathe . . . I can't breathe . . . I can't breathe.*

A cheer rose up around her and she heard men slapping each other on the back. Their words washed over her without meaning, pinning her down. She wasn't sure how long she was there before Zura's feet appeared before her. "Get up."

Cinder pushed one leg under her and then the other. A hand under her arm guided her to her feet. She didn't even have the wherewithal to see who was holding her. She stood swaying, unable to process what had just happened to her.

"I wanted the Luathan girl," grumped the pig-faced man.

"Then you should have opened your purse a little wider," Zura replied. When he continued to look unhappy, she patted his shoulder. "This bidding war has been such a success, we'll be sure to do it again soon."

Again. Bidding war. Cinder wavered on her feet, their enthusiasm breaking across her like a tsunami. There was a brief, hard pressure on her arm. She followed the pressure to find Darsam staring down at her. For a moment, he looked deep into her eyes, his gaze full of promises. Then he was gone.

She would have fallen again, but Farood had stepped in on her other side, holding her arm to keep her upright.

Zura raised her hands, calling for quiet. "In light of recent events, we will have a short break where you may make a new bid or update your existing one with Magian, who is in my office."

They mean to do this tonight? I will face my first patron tonight? Cinder's knees buckled again—the thug's hard grip the only thing keeping her from collapsing.

Her searching gaze found Naiba, who rushed toward her through the crowd, tears streaming down her face. "Cinder!" Naiba wrapped her up in both arms, her grip crushing.

Zura rolled her eyes and called for Farush. "Take her back to the servants' house. If she won't stay, lock her in the cellar."

He jerked the wailing Naiba away, and Cinder watched as he flung her over his shoulder and hauled her toward the servants' house. The men in the room simply parted to let him pass, clearly not at all worried about the sobbing child.

No. They were far too worried about getting their bids in— their bids for Cinder.

CHAPTER SIX

"Y ou used to love to dance as a child," Zura told Cinder as if the memories were pleasant ones. "You will dance those same clannish dances tonight, and you will sing. Because the more money you make, the sooner your time will be done. Am I clear?"

I swear, I will kill you someday. I will put a knife through your black heart and watch the light fade from your eyes, Cinder thought. But she forced herself to say, "Yes, Mother."

Zura turned on her heel and gestured to the open stage. Cinder's face tingled, a thousand needles pricking her at once. She forced herself to walk, one step in front of the other, but it was as if she moved upstream against a great current. Men's deep voices mingled with the merry, tinkling tones of the women., the sound flowing around her, and then continuing on without pause.

All voices fell silent as Cinder passed. She lifted her chin, meeting no one's gaze. Yet she couldn't help but notice Durux waiting beside the platform, a knowing smile on his lips—like she was his already. A trembling started deep inside Cinder, and she faltered a little. A nudge from Farush got her moving again.

Slowly, the men who came to bid peeled away from the others and followed Cinder toward the platform. She climbed the stairs and walked to the center of the dais, the flickering lamplight making the dress flash with her every move. The crimson of the gown deepened to a heart's blood-red.

Everyone was strangely silent, staring at her, just as they had stared at Naiba. Cinder tried to count the men in the room, but there were too many and there wasn't enough time. All of them Idarans. All of them her enemy. Men who would use her for her body while pretending they weren't. And she would be used, while pretending she wasn't. It was a sick madness—one she was drowning in—but there was no escape.

She turned toward the musicians; all the women took turns providing the music. Cinder's dress felt too tight across her chest, and she couldn't seem to catch her breath. She closed her eyes. The music rang out bright and hot, like a midsummer day—the sun beating down on fields of ripe grasses. With the dress shifting against her legs, Cinder began to sway like wind spinning through a village. Women sat at their spindles, men worked the teams, and children's laughter bubbled over the breeze. There were pigs and horses and sheep and dogs. It made a brilliant cacophony of color and texture.

The wind left the village and shot past the crystal-clear waters of a river banked with mossy stones, then bounced over steep hills. Light reflected off the bits of glass in Cinder's dress like sunlight catching the top of a stream. She reached up and took hold of the wind. A heaviness had pushed her limbs down, trapping her in the dark cold, but now the weight lifted. She was the wind, and wind could never be caged.

Cinder surged forward, free to dance as she used to as a child. Now the wind labored over a great mountain, the proud, strong trees causing it to lose its strength. It faltered as it broke upon the glacier, a dirty gray having robbed the snow of its brightness. The wind wandered, lost. But the cold of the place also gave it strength. Soon, it was cutting through deep crevasses, plunging down past a brilliant waterfall, carrying along the mist with it. It rolled over a surface of a pool and rippled it like the bottom of a sandy lake. Then there was no life. Only bare rock and barren emptiness.

Now the wind howled, demanding to be free. It surged over the mountain peak and spilled into the world. Free at last. Free to surge into the never-ending sky. The music faded away.

Cinder had come to a stop in the center of the floor. She could still feel the wind inside her, still see the place her mother had described to her every night before she'd gone to sleep. Cinder tasted the bite of a winter wind on her tongue. She sang of this place, a place of summer's heat and winter's kiss. A place of mighty beauty. When the song ended, she came back into her body slowly and with great reluctance.

Chest heaving with exertion, she looked down at the men, meeting their gazes for the first time. They stared at her, enraptured. She would survive, because they could not own her heart. That was now and would forever be her own.

A single tear rolled down her cheek. Cinder knew it would smear her makeup, leaving a plunging drop of black down her powdered cheek, but she didn't care. Let them know what they were taking from her. Even if only for a moment.

Zura came onto the stage, her razor-sharp stare telling Cinder that her little display had better pay off. She turned to face the men, her smile perfectly fixed in place. "Three generations of clannish women. The newest one is yours for the taking. Any remaining bids will be collected as my men circulate the room. Place your best offer in the chest."

As the men wrote down their final bids, Farush and Farood wove through the crowd to gather the folded bits of fibrous paper. Magian appeared, toting a small table. She stood before it and smartly sorted the bids from highest to lowest as companions wove through the room, bringing drinks to all the men. Cinder ignored them, concentrated on the feeling that she was looking down from somewhere far above.

Magian finished and brought Zura a piece of paper. The older woman's hand trembled a little. When she had finished reading, she lifted her head and visually searched the crowd. Then she turned to Magian, who handed her a small gold box with a ruby in the center of the lid. Zura placed the chest in Cinder's hands. It was just like the box Naiba had held earlier.

"Come with me," Zura said crisply.

Cinder snatched her arm. "Not Durux."

Zura lifted a brow. "He paid handsomely for you. Turning him down is turning down a lot of money."

"Never!" Cinder said vehemently.

Zura grumbled something about how it was easier when her companions were slaves. "Fine."

Cinder counted down as they descended the stairs. She counted as she and Zura wove through the men, who parted as she passed, their gazes disappointed when Cinder didn't stop. *Five.* She recognized some of the men from the last few days. *Four.* But she knew where they were headed. *Three.* She struggled to remain above the thought of any man touching her. *Two.* But when she paused before a man and blinked up at him, suddenly she could breathe again.

"Give him the chest, Cinder," Zura prodded.

Cinder stared at his hard expression. His unwavering gaze. Her mother had said to find a man with kind eyes and deep pockets. Darsam's kind eyes might be a lie, but he was better than Durux. Better than any other man here.

"Give him the chest," Zura said through clenched teeth.

Cinder stretched out her arms and offered the chest to Darsam. He took it from her, his hands never touching hers. He pulled back the lid to reveal a wine-red pomegranate. He removed it from the chest, broke it in half, and popped a handful of seeds into his mouth. The rest of the men filed away.

"She will serve you a private dinner in her rooms," Zura declared, smiling at Cinder. "Her room has—"

"I already ate," Darsam said.

Zura blinked at him. "Drinks, then. Or perhaps you would like to smoke. We have—"

He tossed the rest of the pomegranate at her. "All I need, Mistress Zura, is privacy."

Zura blinked in surprise.

Darsam grasped Cinder's arm and steered her toward the clannish section.

"Remember what we spoke about, Cinder," Zura called to her.

Once in the hallway, Cinder took the lead, steering Darsam to the only empty room in the clannish sector. She wasn't surprised to find it had been freshened up for her. It had false plaster walls, and beams of wood covering a false ceiling, as if she was some sort of exotic bird and this was her cage. Cinder hated it immediately.

She counted to ten, watching as Darsam gently set the gold box on the table. He was back to being quiet and gentle again. "What do you want from me?" she whispered softly so the walls wouldn't hear.

In answer, he stood close and pressed something into her grasp. She opened her fingers enough to catch a glimpse of the object—the ruby earring! Cinder quickly closed her fist again, relief coursing through her. "I'll find a way to take care of this."

"No," he said in a low whisper. "That's not what I meant." He took the ruby earring from Cinder and slipped it into his pocket. Then he stepped closer still, so close there was only the barest slip of air between them. "I promised I would help you. I've paid for your first few nights."

"How is that helping me?" Cinder asked through gritted teeth.

Darsam shifted his weight uncomfortably. "Because I won't take anything from you." He cradled her cheek in his hand. "Except maybe a kiss. Because I know as well as you do that she is watching us right now."

Did he really mean it? Would he truly grant Cinder this reprieve? She glanced at the walls, certain Zura was watching. Then Cinder tipped forward and kissed Darsam. It was her first real kiss. She wasn't sure what she was doing, but she'd seen enough in the House of Night to figure out the basics.

His mouth was soft and sweet, his arms pulling her close. She could feel the hard planes of his body against hers, the stubble of his face scratching at her chin. He released her long enough to blow out the lamps and close the drapes, immersing them in darkness. And then his arms were around her again.

"If she's looking for a show, we have to give it to her," Darsam said quietly. "But I swear I won't take advantage of you."

Cinder began to tremble, the fear coming out of her in little sobs.

"Fire and burning, Cinder, I promise I'm not going to hurt you." He led her to the bed and pulled her under the silken sheets, then wrapped his strong arms around her and held her tight.

"I wish I could believe you," she said in a shaky voice.

"Then let me prove it," Darsam replied.

Cinder curled into a ball and cried silently, her body shuddering with the pain of losing all her of dreams, knowing Darsam couldn't shield her from her fate forever.

CHAPTER SEVEN

Cinder lay in the bed beside Darsam, with his arms wrapped around her, his breath tickling the back of her neck. She counted four seconds for each inhalation and exhalation, steady and even. His arm felt heavy on her side. She hadn't meant to sleep, but she had—deeply and uninterrupted for the first time in days. From the bright light seeping through the drapes, she knew it was morning. She felt lighter somehow. She wasn't free, but her burden didn't seem as heavy as before.

Still wearing the red gown she'd made, she eased from the bed, wincing as the dress tinkled and rustled. Once in the privy, she struggled with the six clasps. She let out a breath of relief when the gown released her. Cinder dropped it to the floor and kicked it into the corner, swearing she'd never wear it again. Then she looked down at her body and traced the lines left by the fitted fabric. Sighing, she pulled on a fine robe and trousers. She tiptoed into the anteroom. She hadn't taken the time to inspect it, but it wasn't so different from her mother's and grandmother's rooms.

Cinder went to the cabinet and opened the drawers, but she couldn't seem to find the pack of wedlock weed. She wasn't even sure why she was looking—it wasn't as if she needed it yet. But that was always the first thing her mother had done whenever she had a patron in her bedroom.

The door slipped open behind Cinder, and she turned to see her grandmother carrying a tray of food. Storm took one look at her, set the tray down, dipped the corner of her apron in a bowl of warm water in the washroom, and hurried over. She wiped under her granddaughter's eyes—Cinder had forgotten about the makeup. "There are things no one can ever take from you," Cinder's grandmother told her firmly. "Memories and emotions are yours, and yours alone. Return to them when you have nowhere else to go."

Cinder gave a tremulous smile. "He was kind to me." She dare not tell Storm anything more, in case Zura or one of her spies was listening.

"If he wasn't, I would kill him," Storm growled. "Not like I have many more years in this world anyway. Might as well use the last of them up all at once."

Panic flooded Cinder's chest "Grandmother, you can't say such things."

Storm cast the walls a challenging smile. "Let her come for me. Let her do her worst." Cinder grabbed her arm, her eyes begging her grandmother to be careful.

"Well then, clean yourself up before you wake him. We're always supposed to be beautiful, after all," her grandmother said bitterly.

Cinder went back to the makeup table and cleaned her face. She counted the strokes as she combed through her hair with a beautiful silver comb, while Storm arranged the food—fruit, and flatbread topped with goat cheese and preserves—on the small table.

"Naiba?" Cinder choked on the name.

"She spent the night with us in the servants' house and rose to clean and bring around the trays. As far as I can tell, she'll be taking your place."

"And I'll be taking hers." Cinder closed her eyes as the reality of her new life tore through her. "I'm not sorry, though."

"You will be," Storm replied, her voice cracking. "Valor only holds you up so long."

Cinder winced. "Why would you say that to me?"

Grimacing, Storm leaned against the table. "I made the brave choice once, the selfless choice. My brother, my people—they all survived because of it. But none of them ever came for me. Now my daughter and granddaughter are paying for my selflessness." She met Cinder's gaze. "No more. Do you understand? You will not suffer anymore because of my decisions."

Breathing hard, Cinder stared at the walls. "Please stop. You'll be punished." Seeing the mulish look her on grandmother's face, Cinder knew she wouldn't. She rooted around for something to distract Storm. "What about the wedlock weed? I can't find any."

Storm wouldn't look at her. Cinder suddenly realized she didn't need to hear the answer. She already knew. "Zura wants me to get pregnant," she gasped. The child of a lord's son would have value in and of itself. "So soon?"

"You'll still be able to perform up to delivery and then a couple days after. Having a baby will only put you out of bedroom work for three, maybe four months. And only for a select number of clients. Many won't care."

Cinder curled her arms protectively around her stomach, tears building in her eyes. "And if I don't get pregnant?"

"If you behave, she'll probably wait until the right patron comes along."

If she behaved. Zura used the children of her companions to keep them in line. Tears slipped from Cinder's eyes as fast as she could wipe them. She determined to find a way into the city to secure her own supply of wedlock weed.

The door behind them flew open. Farush and Farood marched inside and took hold of Storm's arms. Obviously, a spy had reported her. As they dragged her out, she held her up head defiantly, but she didn't fight them.

Zura stood in the doorway, giving Cinder a you'd-better-behave look. Then the mistress left the room and shut the door. Knowing her grandmother would be viciously caned, Cinder counted doubles to distract herself. When she heard sounds coming from the other room, she steeled herself and went into the bedroom. Darsam was pulling on his boots.

"There is breakfast," she said.

"So, numbers . . . that's how you deal with things?"

Cinder winced; she hadn't realized she'd been doing doubles out loud. She felt ashamed. "Numbers never lie. They are . . . always the same. Always right."

Darsam nodded. "You don't belong in a brothel, Cinder. You belong in a university."

"Zura wants me to get pregnant with your child," she whispered.

He froze in the act of tugging on his vest. "Good thing that won't be a possibility." He followed Cinder into the anteroom, then bent down and pressed a kiss to her forehead. "I've paid enough money to have you to myself for two days. Before that is over, I'll get you out of here. I swear it."

Ash's bedroom smelled like a mixture of medicine and makeup as Cinder entered with a tray bearing a bowl of warm water infused with witch hazel. Her grandmother lay on the bed. Her mother sat before the makeup dresser.

"We need to do your makeup," Ash reminded Cinder softly.

Cinder nodded as she set down the tray and replaced the dried-out rags on her grandmother's back with fresh ones. She counted the welts again. Fifty of them. She handed her grandmother a cup of willow-bark-and-arnica tea. Storm quickly drank the bitter concoction and then collapsed back against the bed. "Did you manage to get anything stronger?"

Cinder placed the bowl of witch hazel on the nightstand so her grandmother could reach it. "No. Zura has everything locked down tight."

Her grandmother gestured to her robes. "Will you please get Holla's carving?"

Cinder pulled out the simple carving, which was dark brown from being touched for so many years. It was a beaver, something Cinder had never seen in real life, cut perfectly in half. Holla had carried it with her everywhere. Cinder remembered the story—how Storm and Holla's brother, Otec, had carved it for her aunt. Holla had taken it with her from the clanlands when she was kidnapped. Taunting her slurred speech, one of her captors had cut the carving in half.

Holla had left the other piece, certain her brother would find it. Then they would both have a piece.

"Do you think he ever found it—the other half of the carving?" Cinder asked.

Storm tucked the little carving into the palm of her hand. "I don't know." Her gaze was distant. "Otec had a chance to save us. He had chased us halfway across the clanlands. But he had to make a choice—save the captives or save the clanlands. Trying to be brave, I told him to save the clanlands. He listened to me. Why did he listen to me?"

Storm broke down in sobs. Cinder had rarely seen her grandmother cry. "I would tell him that I will never forgive him," Storm said, answering her own question. "That he should have built an army himself and come to free us. But he never did. He left us here to rot."

Cinder felt her mother's hand on her shoulders. "Come, we'll get ready in your rooms."

Knowing how much her grandmother hated for anyone to see her cry, Cinder squeezed her grandmother's hand and followed her mother into her rooms.

Ash scooted over so Cinder could sit by her on the bench. Her mother taught her how to apply the makeup. Before they finished, Zura made the rounds with the jewelry. Magian chose a sapphire headdress and bangles that attached to a ring by a slim chain to go with Cinder's royal-blue dress, which lacked the faceted glass of the last dress, though it was made after the same fashion. She wore the gold sandals she'd made, covered in sparkling bits of cut glass.

Then it was time to perform the dances. On the stage with the other eleven clannish women, under the golden lights of the lamps, Cinder felt her anger rising. She didn't want to be here, on display for these men. Then her gaze caught on Darsam's face. He gave her a solemn nod and she realized maybe she could dance for him.

So she danced with the other companions, counting out the beats of the music. It was an Idaran dance, with movement in the wrists, hips, and shoulders. It was playful and light, meant to wash the men's cares away. When Cinder finished, she and Darsam went back to her small dining room. He settled on the large cushions while she brought them a tray filled with all the foods she'd always longed to try, but never been allowed to. They ate for a time, while he told her about his day—mindless things to bore anyone who might be listening.

When Cinder had eaten until she thought her stomach might burst, Darsam leaned in and asked. "Is there somewhere safe to talk?"

He followed her to her pivot door, and they slipped outside. She led him to Holla's flowers, where she knelt carefully and began to pull at the weeds that had managed to spring up. "My aunt is buried here. Her name was Holla. She came over with my grandmother from the clanlands. She was the one who raised me. She never learned to speak Idaran very well. But she could clean and she worked hard." Here, with the moonlight and the smell of the soil all around her, Cinder almost felt like her aunt might be here, watching over them.

"How did she die?"

Cinder sighed. "In her sleep. She was . . . different. Things that are easy for other people were hard for her, but that just meant she worked harder than anyone else I knew. Some things that were hard for other people were easy for her—things like happiness and kindness."

Darsam knelt beside Cinder. "Is it safe to talk here?"

"We never know. That's one of the things that gives Zura so much power."

Cinder tipped her head to the side and touched his thick hair. "I've never known men who didn't shave their scalps." His hair was thick and soft, with a slight wave. Then she touched his clean-shaven cheek and gave a little smile. "And you shave your face."

"Clanmen shave neither."

She studied him. "Which Darsam is the real one—the cocky spoiled son of the lord, or the gentle, quiet man?"

"Don't you know?" he said sadly.

Whenever he was on display, he was loud and cocky. But with her . . . "I don't think I like the Darsam who cares more about his chariot team and his reputation."

"What about the one you see right now?"

She pressed her hand over his heart, which thrummed steadily beneath her hand. "That man, I think I could respect." It was the most she could give.

Darsam reached out to run his fingers down her hair and then along her cheek. "Skin is skin," he murmured. He placed his hand over hers, which still rested on his chest. "Your heart beats the same as mine."

Cinder looked into his eyes, wondering what he was trying to tell her.

"If we're so much alike, why am I a lord's son and you a slave?"

"Because the law says so," she replied.

"My father is trying to change that law. Has been for years. We've managed to put most of the slavers and brothels out of business. Zura is one of the last holding out, but she's badly in debt to Jatar. The little game she played last night was her last-ditch attempt to get out of it."

Cinder had suspected as much. She looked into Darsam's eyes. "And you . . . you help your father?"

"While we wait for his legal maneuvers to pay off, my men and I get as many people out as we can in . . . less legal ways. I play the cad, when I'm really gathering information to help shut down a brothel. If everything is perfectly legal, my tribesmen and I smuggle as many girls out as we can. The ones who don't have a home to return to we find a place in the Adrack."

"And Zura is perfectly legal," Cinder guessed.

"I broke into her records during the night," Darsam said. Cinder hadn't known that—hadn't even known he had left her. "She's meticulous to a fault," he continued.

"What does all this have to do with Jatar? What do *I* have to do with Jatar?"

For a moment, Darsam looked tired. "We don't know that yet. We've been following Jatar and Durux for months, hoping to catch one of them breaking a law so we could send them to a prison mine and shut their businesses down. Therefore, we took note when Durux started following you—I took note. I watched you, Cinder, moving from one business to the next, day after day, week after week. I'd never seen such dogged determination.

"So when one of my spies overheard Durux plotting to kill you, I rushed to the glass-maker's shop to make sure you were safe." Darsam gave a bitter laugh. "Imagine my surprise when Sadira pushed you in front of my own chariot."

Durux had hired Sadira to try to kill Cinder? But why? How would her death benefit the smuggler? Cinder could feel Darsam's heart pounding beneath her palm. "You knew me before I ever met you," she said.

He smiled. "I had to play the spoiled lord's son when I wanted nothing more than to haul you into my chariot and take you to safety. I should have—fire and burning, I should have. But Durux was sending me a message. He knew we were watching him. And somehow he knew I was interested in you."

Cinder's mind snagged on one word. "Interested?"

Darsam reached out to touch her hair. "Silver and gold— that's the first thing I thought of when I saw you. So smart. So determined. I wanted to know you."

"If you're so keen to help me, to know me, why take the earring from my mother?"

"Too many women back out at the last minute if they don't have something at stake. It weeds out the ones who aren't determined. Running a smuggling operation is expensive. I already squandered my inheritance. But there are still people to pay off, supplies to purchase, men who have to eat and need a place to sleep. None of it can be linked back to my father."

Cinder rose to her feet and circled the garden. There were tall trees and benches and dozens and dozens of flowers and bushes of vibrant colors, all of them come to life since the rains the night before. She paused beside each one, trailing her fingers along the soft petals.

"This is Havesh's flower." Cinder crossed the paving stones and stood before another flower. "This is Marva's." She continued on, pointing out each plant and naming the woman beneath it.

"Where's yours?" Darsam asked, clearly not understanding.

"I don't have one yet," Cinder whispered.

She paused before a desert rose. A single bud had opened, bright coral with a yellow center. Cinder knelt next to it, not caring about her robes, and breathed in the fresh, citrusy scent as she remembered the woman beneath it.

Darsam knelt beside her. "Zura plants flowers in the memory of those who have died?"

Cinder huffed. "No. She plants the flowers over their corpses to remind us what happens when we step out of line." She looked up at him. "I don't want to join them."

He reached down and pulled her to her feet. "Determination will only get you so far. You have to have plans. And more than a little luck. I have both."

"What do you mean?"

He leaned forward, his mouth inches from her ear, but then there was the sound of someone pushing through the brush and laughing. They both stiffened as a man and woman appeared. One of the Luathan women nodded to Cinder as she passed. Then the couple disappeared into the darkness. Soon, the sounds of passion floated back to Cinder's ears.

Darsam took her hand and led her toward her room. "What did you mean before?" she asked him.

Only when they were tucked safely in the dark of the room with her in his arms did he answer, "Be ready. Tonight."

"For what?"

"To escape." He wouldn't say more as he left her in the darkness alone.

CHAPTER EIGHT

Cinder didn't mean to fall asleep again, but suddenly someone was shaking her shoulder. A shadowed, cloaked face hovered above her. She gasped and started to scramble back, but a hand gripped her.

"Come with me, quickly."

It was her grandmother. Behind Storm stood another figure—Cinder's mother. Ash pushed Cinder's cloak, headscarf, and veil into her hands. As she followed her matriarchs out the pivot door, Cinder asked, "What's going on?"

"We're going home," Ash answered in a half-whisper.

"To the clanlands? We can't—we'll be caught. We'll be killed."

"There are worse things than dying," Storm said in a voice heavy with emotion. "Will you too watch your daughter be forced to play the harlot?"

"We're not going to die," Ash added quickly. "Now come on."

Cinder planted her feet. "What about Naiba? If I leave, she will be forced to take my place." The thought filled Cinder with horror.

Her mother shook her head. "I've paid for three of us, not four."

Cinder spun on her heel and ran for the servants' house before her mother or grandmother could stop her. She counted her steps up to the attic, slipped down the row of beds, and shook Naiba's arm. When the girl sat up, Cinder held a finger to her lips. Naiba followed her to the kitchen, where Storm waited.

In shock, Naiba looked around. "You're escaping."

"You cannot stay behind," Storm said, her shoulders set in the moonlight. "They'll kill you for not informing them."

Naiba's eyes were enormous in her head. "A girl my age ran—they cut off her ear."

Storm pulled a knife from her cloak. "I don't want to kill you, child. But I will if I have to."

Cinder took a step toward her grandmother, her mouth open to protest.

Naiba spoke before she could. "So I die either way. I might as well die with the hope of escape."

The four of them crossed the deserted courtyard, heading for the back gate. Ash pushed the gate open and they hurried out. Gathering herself to go after them, Cinder looked back and saw the guard's boots sticking out from beneath the rose bushes. She couldn't find it in herself to feel sorry for him.

Loaded with large clay pots, a wagon waited in the shadows of a building. A hooded figure sat in the driver's seat, while Darsam flipped open a trapdoor near the back of the wagon. Beneath the wagon bed and running the length of it was a secret compartment. Cinder swallowed hard as she stared at the confined space.

"Why are there four of you?" Darsam asked as he motioned for the women to get inside the compartment.

"Cinder insisted," growled Storm.

"We won't have enough horses for her once we're outside the city," Darsam explained.

Cinder let out a little huff. "Well, I'm not leaving her behind."

"We can leave her at the Sand Snake," suggested the driver. "Try to get her out later."

"Naiba?" Cinder said questioningly.

"Can we trust them?" the girl asked.

Cinder hesitated. "Yes," she said finally, feeling Darsam's gaze on her.

He gave a quick nod, then helped Ash and Storm into the secret compartment. Naiba shimmied herself in.

"Have you been planning this since you met my grandmother at the Sand Snake?" Cinder asked, knowing a part of her was delaying the inevitable.

"That was Ashar, not me." Darsam gestured to the driver, who was keeping a lookout. It was the man Cinder had seen in the House of Night. "Get inside," urged Darsam

Cinder stared into the dark, cramped space. Her breaths came too fast, her heart racing. "I . . . I'm not sure I can."

"Use the numbers," Darsam told her.

Cinder glanced at him, wishing it were light out so she could read his expression. She positioned herself between her mother and Naiba, then closed her eyes and slid into the cramped space, which smelled of sour wine. Cinder rolled onto her stomach and heard Darsam latch the door behind them. She whimpered as the wagon creaked forward, shuddering over the flagstones.

Her mother took one of Cinder's hands, Naiba the other. Cinder closed her eyes and counted 1,802 seconds before the wagon came to a halt. There was a little sliver missing from the wood, big enough for her to see an abandoned building, moonlight reflecting off the windows like dead eyes. On the other side was the Sand Snake.

Cinder squeezed Naiba's hand. "You can trust Darsam. He's a good man."

The girl took in a deep breath. "I never had a chance to thank you—what you did for me . . ."

Something swelled in Cinder's throat, but she managed to say, "Your name is Yula again."

The trapdoor opened and fresh air rushed inside the compartment. Cinder gasped, fighting the urge to haul herself out of the small space. Suddenly, she realized she would probably never see Naiba again. Her friend seemed to come to the same conclusion, for they reached for each other at the same time. As they embraced each other, silent sobs racked Naiba.

"Cinder, I'm sorry, but we must hurry," Darsam whispered.

"I love you, Cinder," Naiba said softly. "I will always love you."

Then she let go and hauled herself out of the small compartment. Cinder had time to see the basement door open before Darsam shut the trapdoor again. She tried to start doubles, but the slippery numbers fell out of her grasp before she could put them in order. There was a hasty conversation outside, and then they were moving once more.

There was more room now—almost enough to breathe. "Are they the only ones helping us?" Cinder asked Ash, desperate to distract herself. She had hoped the stolen earring would be enough to hire a dozen men.

"The rest are waiting outside the city with horses," Ash answered as she rose up on her elbows to peer outside. A stray bit of light streaming from the taverns revealed scratches on her mother's arms. "Is he dead? The guard?" Cinder asked.

Ash glanced at the welts. "He got what he deserved." Cinder felt a sharp pain in her belly. There was no going back for them, not now. "Once we reach the edge of the desert, we'll trade the horses for camels," her mother explained.

"All this for one earring?" Cinder asked softly.

Her mother took Cinder's hand and pushed it into her pocket. Feeling the hard, smooth stones with metal prongs, Cinder jerked her hand back. "I took the whole set," Ash told her. "It will buy us passage through the Adrack Desert and a ship to take us to the clanlands."

"We're finally going home." Cinder's grandmother's voice caught at the words.

Thinking of the key always dangling from a chain around Zura's neck, Cinder asked her mother, "How did you get the jewels in the first place?"

Ash chuckled softly. "Have you forgotten who taught you to pick a lock?"

In the dark and cloistered wagon bed, Ash reached out and took hold of Cinder's hand.

"We're going to make it," Cinder said. She'd never ventured beyond the city walls. Never seen the fields and orchards up close. Never known life beyond the never-ending heat and the taste of sand on her tongue. She was not sorry to leave. The wagon lumbered to a stop, and she imagined the city's tall wall, lamplight casting a flickering glow over the city.

"The gates are closed for the night. Come back at first light," called an authoritative voice.

"Wife won't like me not showing up—she already thinks me a drunkard and a fool." Ashar's words were slurred. "Not that it isn't true, mind you, but I cannot abide the nagging. What say we bypass the rules and let an old man home to his bed, eh?"

"Come back in the morning," said the watchman, clearly annoyed.

Ashar was silent a beat before he tried again. "Where's old Grez? He always lets me through on the nights I drink."

Someone growled in frustration. "Oh, he does, does he? We'll just check your cargo and then you can be on your way."

Cinder hardly dared to breathe as footsteps sounded around the wagon. Above her, she could hear the empty pots shift as someone moved them around. "The bed of this wagon seems far too high," commented one of the watchmen. Cinder longed to peek out the sliver, but she dared not even move as the lamplight swung around, filling the tight space with enough light that she could see her body for the first time in over an hour. She heard the brush of flesh on wood and then a catch gave. The trapdoor swung open to reveal the hard face of the watchman holding the lamp.

Darsam jumped down in front of the women, driving the watchman back with a great black sword. "Run!" Darsam cried. From the front of the wagon came the sounds of clanging swords. One of the watchmen shouted for help.

Cinder grabbed hold of the ledge above her and pulled herself out of the wagon. A breeze touched her clammy clothes, and suddenly she could breathe again. She reached back into the darkness to help her grandmother to her feet, but Ash slapped a knife into Cinder's hand and shoved her. "Go!"

They sprinted into the empty space between the city wall and the buildings. The watchman's shouts had brought out people along the walkway. Three men pounded down the stone stairs, swords in hand. Two of the men went to help the pair fighting Darsam and Ashar. The third sprinted after the women. Cinder heard his steps coming closer, felt the skin between her shoulder blades prickle with his presence. A hand grabbed the back of her cloak. She ducked out of it and kept running. Only a second later, the man's hand caught her hair.

She screamed as he jerked her around and pinned her against and the wall, then placed his curved sword against her throat. He blinked in surprise when he saw her face. "You're one of Darsam's girls?"

Could he possibly be among the men Darsam had paid to look the other way? Breathing shallowly through her nose to keep her exposed throat as small as possible, Cinder breathed out, "Yes."

Before he could respond, a hand wrapped around him from behind, a knife point pressed to his neck. "Kill her and you die too," Ash hissed. Cinder had never seen her mother so furious. Storm was there, too.

For a breathless moment, they all stood like that, knives and swords and death only a twitch away. "I have no desire to kill any of you," said the man, withdrawing his sword a little. Ash backed away as he did.

For a split second, Cinder met the watchman's eyes. She was still in range of his sword, while he was relatively safe from the knife. He could have swung his blade at her—could have ended her life. Instead, he growled in frustration and pointed. "Run!"

Barely able to believe he'd let them go, Cinder pivoted and ran without looking back. They would have to find a place to hide. Tomorrow, perhaps, they could try to find Darsam or one of his tribesmen smugglers at the Sand Snake and sneak out of the city. But just as the three women turned up a street, they found themselves facing two hulking shapes holding cudgels. The door to a building on their right flew open, the light outlining a figure that pointed at them.

"Get them!" Zura cried.

Cinder, Storm, and Ash whirled around to run. But the other guard had caught up to them and now trapped them between himself and Zura's thugs. Heart pounding, Cinder shot the first guard a pleading look—after all, he'd let them go once—but he glanced at Zura and her thugs and reluctantly lifted his sword. Cinder whirled in a circle, searching for a side door or an alley. Something.

"I don't mind killing you, Ash," Zura said. "But then, maybe I won't. Maybe I'll just kill your mother. Her usefulness is about at an end anyway."

"By the Balance," Ash said softly, "there is no justice in the world." She tossed her knife onto the flagstone.

Refusing to give up so quickly, Cinder looked for Darsam. But from this distance, and with more shadows than light, she couldn't tell which of the two smugglers was which. One of the guard's swords connected, and a smuggler grunted and went down on one knee. Cinder clenched her twenty-eight teeth so hard she thought they might shatter. Reluctantly, the smuggler dropped his sword. One watchman stood guard over him, while the other went to join the two men fighting the second smuggler.

Now Darsam was outnumbered three to one. "Put it down," said one of the guards. "You know it's over."

"Fine." Cinder recognized Darsam's voice. He sounded almost bored. He was all right! Her jaw relaxed. "It's not like I won't be out in the morning," he drawled. The watchmen forced him to the ground.

With no other option, Cinder released her death grip and dropped her knife. Her hand ached as the blood rushed back in.

"I told you, Captain Hazev," Zura called to one of the men tying up Darsam, "that some of my slaves were planning an escape. I told you Darsam was paying off watchmen to look the other way."

Cinder sucked in a breath. How could Zura have known?

"It seems you were right, Mistress Zura," a man called back. "Grez will be dealt with, I assure you."

Zura looked around. "There is another girl—a young Luathan. Where is she?"

"She wasn't with them in the wagon," Hazev said as he came toward them. He was the man who had opened the hidden door in the wagon.

At least Naiba—Yula—was safe.

"I want her found," Zura barked. "I'll deal with the rest of them myself."

"She's freeborn," Ash said before the watchman could respond. Her searching hand found Cinder's upper arm and pulled her in front of him, tipping the side of her head toward the light for proof. "Let her go."

Laz turned to Zura. "Is this true?"

Zura's shadowed gaze fixed on Cinder. "Freeborn she may be, but she consorted with criminals to steal my property—jewels and slaves alike. One of my men is dead."

"Not by any of our hands," Ash said a little too smoothly.

"This girl stole nothing. I took them." Cinder's grandmother removed the jewels from Ash's pockets and threw them on the ground at Zura's feet in disgust. "As payment for the years you kept me against my will."

"You don't have any will," Zura hissed as she crouched to scoop up the jewels. "Tie them all up and take them to the cellar." Another watchman joined the group, and the two men came forward, along with Farush and Farood, to tie the captives' hands behind their backs.

Laz turned to his commanding officer. "Sir, they have no legal right to take an Idaran citizen."

"Fine," Hazev said.

Laz pulled Cinder out of Farush's grasp. "You can take your property, but the girl is under arrest. She's a prisoner of the city watch now."

Zura shrugged. "Fine." Cinder wondered why she wasn't fighting harder.

"And the smugglers?" Laz asked.

"Bring them as well," said Captain Hazev.

Storm wrenched free of Farood's grasp and came to rest her forehead against Cinder's. The firelight caught the shadows in her panicked eyes, twisting them into grotesque shapes. "Listen to me, Cinder. You survive the mine. Survive in any way you can. And when you get out, leave this province—leave Idara. Don't look back. Never come back. Promise me. Swear it."

Then Storm was wrenched away. Cinder stumbled after her, but the watchmen held her tight. She stared helplessly as her grandmother and mother were dragged away and pushed to the floor of the chariot.

"Cinder," Ash called in desperation.

"Swear it!" Storm said. "Swear you won't come back!"

Cinder didn't answer as the shadows swallowed her grandmother whole.

CHAPTER NINE

The bolt across the heavy door groaned and the door flew open. Darsam was unceremoniously dumped inside. He winced as the door slammed behind him and the bolt slid home. Cinder scrambled to his side. One large bruise on his cheek, one split and swollen lip, one eye nearly swollen shut.

"Darsam," she said breathlessly. She didn't know how to help him, or even where to start.

"They're always so pleased to see me when I come back." He took a shallow breath. "I don't think they even managed to break my ribs this time."

She pushed her hair off her sweaty forehead and tucked the strands behind her ears. "Tell me what to do."

He shifted to look at her in the dim light coming from the tiny, high window. It was daytime. "Nothing's broken, just bruises and cuts. A week or two and I'll be fine."

Cinder got the bucket of water from the corner and sat again, then ripped off a piece of her undergarment and dipped it into the questionable-looking water. She began gently cleaning Darsam's face, counting the strokes to calm herself. "Luckily for us," he said with a wince, "I bribed one of the guards to put me in with you."

"You could bribe them to put you in my cell, but not to stop them from beating you?"

He gave a little shrug. "It was one or the other."

"Laz is one of your men?"

"He went to inform my father we've been caught. I'm not sure what happened to Grez."

Cinder concentrated on removing the caked blood from Darsam's eyebrow. "What about Yula?"

"Yula?"

"Naiba."

"The girl from last night? She'll be fine. It's your mother and grandmother we need to worry about." Darsam let out a long exhale.

Cinder had to count up to ten and back down before she could breathe normally. "Can I ask you something?"

He met her gaze. "Cinder, I don't think I could deny you anything."

She felt herself warming from the inside out. "No matter what happens to me, will you look after my mother and grandmother? Find a way to free them."

He grunted. "I come from a long line of smugglers. My cousin is Rycus, consort to Goddess Nelay. Ashar is one of my uncles. We'll get them out."

Fire and burning, this man was powerful. "Where will they take me?" Cinder asked.

"You'll appear before the magistrates. They'll decide. But don't worry too much. I'll pull some strings."

Not wanting to imagine how Idaran magistrates would sentence the daughter of clannish slaves, Cinder carefully wiped away the blood that had run down Darsam's neck and chest. As she lifted his shirt to get better access, she had to try very hard not to stare at the perfect muscles of his abdomen. "So you're a regular in jail?"

He smirked and then winced as if he regretted it. "My father won't let them throw me in a mine or a slave ship, so they take their punishment the only way they can. Luckily, they don't dare break anything. Most of the time."

Cinder wiped at the dried blood in the corner of his mouth. "You're not who I thought you were."

Darsam grunted. "I hate being seen as a fop. Hate pretending to be something I'm not. But then I'm sure you know all about pretending."

She stared at this man, handsome, rich, and powerful, who trolled the streets looking for slaves and prostitutes to save. "Why help me? What's in it for you?"

His tongue slipped out the corner of his mouth, probing the split in his lip. "No one has ever asked me that." He stared up at the ceiling. "Because of my stepmother, I suppose. She taught me that the first test of a man is how he treats those who are weak. The second test is if he teaches those who are weak to become strong."

Staring at him in awe, Cinder felt tears pricking her eyes. "Because of me, the slavers and brothel owners will know who you are and what you're doing now. You won't be able to help any more of us."

Darsam reached out to cup her face in his hands. "I couldn't let them hurt you. Not you."

Heat spread from his touch, and Cinder remembered him mentioning an interest in her. "I'm sorry I didn't treat you well before," she said. "I didn't know."

"I didn't mind. Mostly, I couldn't believe you could be surrounded by so much evil for so long and not be jaded."

"Holla taught me," Cinder whispered. "And my mother and grandmother shielded me."

Darsam's thumb moved to gently brush under her eyes. "You look tired."

"I haven't slept much. I was too worried."

He tugged on her hand. "I make a good cushion." She blushed and he chuckled softly. "It's not the first time, Cinder."

She bit her lip. "What do you want from me, Darsam?"

"Whatever you're willing to give."

"I don't . . . I don't know what that is." It was obvious he had feelings for her; she just wasn't sure she returned them.

"You don't owe me anything, Cinder. You don't owe *anyone* anything."

Right answer. She smiled and rested her head on his chest. But she didn't sleep, because the warmth that had spread from his hand was now coursing through her whole body. She felt alive in ways she'd never experienced before. Wondering if Darsam was feeling the same emotions, she glanced up at him and noted a little furrow between his brows as he stared at the ceiling. "What's wrong?"

He stroked her arm with the back of his fingers. "Normally my father's men would have come for me by now."

Cinder couldn't help but think they were missing something—something bigger that was at play—but she couldn't imagine what. Just then, the cell door was flung open. Despite his injuries, Darsam was on his feet before Cinder could turn to face the door.

Two guards stood there, one with his sword already drawn and pointed at Darsam. "Get the girl."

Cinder shrank back, perfectly willing to stay in this smelly room for the rest of her life if it meant she didn't have to face the magistrates.

"Where are my father's men?" Darsam complained, all arrogance again. "Why haven't I been released yet?"

The guard didn't answer as one man came for Cinder. She backed away, somehow knowing that if she was separated from Darsam, something bad would happen. "No. I don't—"

The guard grabbed for her hand, but Darsam was quicker and jerked her behind him. "I want my father notified. Now."

The two remaining guards drew their swords and advanced. Darsam backed away until Cinder was pressed between him and a wall that smelled of piss.

"Girl, come with me. Now!" said one of the guards.

She didn't move. Neither did Darsam. "Hurt me, and you risk my father's wrath."

The guard slid forward, the arc of his sword poised to strike. "Laz has been . . . detained. Your false-lord father doesn't even know you're here."

"He'll figure it out eventually," Darsam said, his voice sharp now.

The guard stepped just a little closer and sneered. "By then it will be too late."

"Girl," the other guard barked, "come out now or we'll run him through."

Feeling smaller than a mouse, Cinder slid out from behind Darsam and took a step toward the men. Darsam's hand snaked out, grabbing her. "Cinder!"

"We don't have a choice, Darsam."

His eyes sparked with anger. She pulled free and took a step toward the men. They grabbed her arms and dragged her out of the cell, then slammed the door.

Cinder's last glimpse of Darsam was of him rushing the door. She winced as he pounded it with the flat of his hand and yelled, "Cinder!"

The sky was a uniform gray, the promise of rain heavy in the air. But the clouds held back, waiting. Cinder counted seconds as she was taken by chariot to the center of the city, into the Justice Building. There were lines of people that looked worse off than her. Missing teeth and missing shoes and simply missing, like something that should be there wasn't. They were coming and going—mostly going. One man shouted, demanding to see a different magistrate, refusing to be taken to the prison mine. His spit flew all over Cinder as the guards dragged him past.

Wiping her face with her sleeve, she tried to keep her wits about her, but she was so hungry and so very tired. She bypassed the line and the guards handed her off to another man, who held a scroll. He looked her over. "All the exits are guarded. Try to run, and your feet will be bound and you will be caned. Do you understand?"

Head down, Cinder nodded.

"Do you understand?" he asked again, loudly.

She jumped a little and realized he hadn't been looking at her. "I understand." She almost called him "Mother," but caught herself just in time.

The man pivoted on his heel. Cinder hurried after him, glancing back in surprise as the two watchmen who had escorted her into the building left without a word. She entered a room and froze, every instinct demanding that she run.

Zura's hair was perfectly braided, her makeup expertly applied. She wore sky-blue robes of excellent quality, but no jewelry. As Cinder entered the room, Zura turned to her with a haughty expression. Behind the woman stood Jatar and Durux. The younger man's ears were pink with excitement.

In that moment, Cinder knew she had made a mistake in leaving Darsam. Because whatever these three had planned for her, it was worse than a prison mine.

Unable to help it, she ran. She made it past the guards, whose shouts streamed after her. She burst into the open and headed down the center of the street, guards trailing behind her. If she could just outrun them, she could hide, sneak out of the city. Leave Arcina and Idara far behind.

But then arms wrapped around her, wrenching her to the side as she fell headlong into the damp paving stones. Her shoulder dragged along the street. She heard the fabric shred and felt the grit tearing away her skin.

Clawing at the guards' hands, she tried to scrabble free, but more arms hauled her up. One of the guards brushed himself off, muttering curses. The other guard teased him about tearing another uniform. The first guard shot back that his uniforms were torn because at least he was fast enough to catch the prisoners.

It was as if Cinder wasn't a real person. They didn't care that she was dying inside. They caned her—five quick, merciless strikes that had her curled up on her side, grunting with each blow. Then they hauled her back in front of the magistrate, making her stand in a little box with her hands and feet in chains so she could only take short steps.

The magistrate squinted at her like he had bad vision and couldn't quite make her out. The man with the scroll said, "Cinder, ward to Mistress Zura, has been charged with the theft of a diamond-and-ruby jewelry set, as well as attempting to steal slaves and cause an uprising. There is also the murder of a guard, most likely by poisoning."

The magistrate leaned back. "Did you do these things?"

"No," Cinder said simply.

"Then why does Mistress Zura say you did?"

Cinder ground her teeth. "Because she is a liar."

The magistrate gave Zura a questioning stare.

"I have witnesses," the woman said evenly.

He nodded for her to continue. She waved at someone in the back of the room. Limping, Laz came forward. His face was swollen and bruised, and he was hunched over as if in pain. Cinder gasped. This man had not sustained any injuries last night. And his wounds looked recent—a bandage at his head sported bright blood.

"Speak," the magistrate said.

He hesitated, casting Durux a nervous look. The slaver simply tapped the knife hilt at his waist. Laz closed his eyes. "My name is Captain Laz. I witnessed this girl, along with the other slaves, as they tried to sneak out the city gate."

"Magistrate," Cinder said breathlessly. "This man wasn't injured last night. They've done something to him. You have to help him."

"So you admit you were with the other slaves, trying to escape?" the magistrate asked as he marked something on a scroll before him.

"Yes, but—"

"Thank you, Captain Laz, you may go." The magistrate looked at his assistant. "What were the other charges?"

"Murder and theft," the man said promptly.

"Ah yes." The magistrate gestured to Zura. "I assume you have witnesses to these charges as well."

Zura snapped her fingers. Magian stepped forward and reported that Cinder had picked the lock to the jewelry cabinets.

"You witnessed this?" the man asked.

Magian shook her head. "No, but the girl has a history of picking locks."

"And as to the murder?" the magistrate asked.

Zura hesitated, but Cinder could see it was all an act. "As to that, we have no witnesses as yet, but—"

"Until such time as one comes forward, the charges have no merit." He turned his attention to Cinder, studying her as silence rang through the room. "The court only needs the word of three witnesses to prove your guilt. You've already admitted to trying to escape. Can you provide three witnesses to discredit the accusations of thievery?"

"Why should I need to escape when I am free?" Cinder said. "As for witnesses, my mother and grandmother will tell you that

I didn't even know about the escape until they came for me that night. And I never stole any jewels."

"I can attest that the girl is rather adept at picking locks," Durux said smoothly. "I've seen her in action."

Just hearing the man's voice made Cinder cringe. "I haven't done anything wrong."

The magistrate waved as if erasing her words. "By your own admission, you went along with a slave escape instead of trying to prevent it. That alone is enough for five years in the prison mine. In this case, I find you guilty of the theft as well as your considerable debt. You will serve fifteen years in the mines, digging for luminash with the rest of the criminals."

Cinder's legs gave out. She would be thirty-two by the time she was free—if she survived.

"There is more," Zura said dramatically.

The magistrate shot her an annoyed look. She nodded to Magian, who brought out the ponderous ledger. The bookkeeper tried to hand it to the magistrate, but he waved for her to hand it to the scribe, who looked over the figures with more interest than he had anything else. "It's an accounting of the cost of raising the girl, as well as companion expenses."

The magistrate clicked his tongue impatiently. "And?"

The scribe's lips moved as if he was reading aloud. "I would need more time to check the numbers, but according to this, Cinder has incurred a debt of more than five hundred attalics."

"No! It was 120—the cost of raising me," Cinder said, her panic rising.

Zura gave her a smug look. "In addition to the cost of the gowns you stole, there's the purchase price of your slave— Naiba—who is still missing." Cinder felt a moment of acute relief that at least her friend was safe. "Then there is the cost of the fabric and jewels for your outfitting as a companion, valued at seventy-five attalics—"

Fear rose up, choking Cinder. "I didn't buy any jewelry!"

Zura went on as if Cinder hadn't even spoken. "Plus the cost of throwing her auction party. She's well over five hundred attalics in debt."

"Is this true?" the magistrate asked.

The clerk nodded. "It's all very well documented, sir."

"But the dress wasn't even for me!" Cinder cried. "It was for Naiba! And the jewels I wore were Zura's! As was the cost of the auction—it was all for Naiba, not me."

"Dozens of well-placed men already have contracts with the girl, and of course I have her own signed contract to become a companion for the House of Night." Zura handed some documents to the clerk.

The man perused them and then nodded. "It's all in order, sir."

The magistrate made an unhappy sound low in his throat. "And I suppose you want to enact the debtor's law rather than see her spend time in prison?"

"Would it not be kinder to live in my mansion, entertaining the good men of the city—men such as yourself?" Zura smiled her gentle smile. "As you are well aware, Your Honor, anyone more than four hundred attalics in debt, with no hopes of paying it off, loses his or her freeborn status. It is my right to take this girl as my slave."

"You monster!" Cinder gasped. Zura glanced at her sideways, a little smirk playing on her lips. Cinder closed her eyes with a sick realization and mumbled, "This was your plan all along." She had been a fool to believe the woman might give her a chance to make her own way—to become her own woman. But Cinder's mother had known better. So she'd enacted her own desperate plan . . . and played right into Zura's hands.

Cinder turned to the magistrate. "Please—I'd rather dig rocks for the rest of my life."

The magistrate passed his hand down his face. He shook his head. "Zura is right. The debtor's law allows her to take you as her slave to compensate her the loss of—"

"I have worked myself to the bone my entire life serving her! And my debt is always higher than my wages! The people she's brought before you are her servants—of course they're lying for her. You can't—"

"Her time and property," the magistrate spoke over her. "And as such, I revoke your freeborn status and make you a slave." He pushed up from his chair. "Scribe, see that the papers are redrawn. Have an official marker sent for and change her tattoo."

Cinder ran toward him. Zura motioned to her thugs and they rushed forward, gripping both of her arms.

Cinder fought and kicked. "I am freeborn! I am an Idaran! You can't do this! Please!"

But the magistrate ignored her, and the thugs were accustomed to screaming, desperate women. They dragged her from the room.

CHAPTER TEN

The sides of her head throbbing from her new tattoos, Cinder was dragged back into the cloudy daylight. In the distance thunder rumbled. "Go fetch the chariot," Zura said to Farush. He went to do as she had bid.

A squinting Jatar rounded on them, one hand resting on his sword hilt. Durux stood beside him. The man's chariot pulled up behind him, the driver staring Zura and her thugs down.

"The girl comes with us," Jatar said.

Cinder came out of her stupor and attempted to pull away from Farood. His grip tightened, four fingernails digging into the soft flesh under her arm.

Zura's gaze narrowed. "That was never part of the agreement."

"Hand her over," Durux said.

Now Cinder started fighting in earnest. Farood put her into a submission hold, but being barely able to move didn't stop her from struggling.

Zura looked over the three slavers. "Jatar, she is my slave now—"

"You are in debt to me far more than four hundred attalics. Shall we go back into the magistrate and make you my slave as well?"

Zura's face went ashen. "Which is why I had to ensure that Cinder became my slave. I already have contracts out for patrons well in excess of our agreed-upon payment. Her worth over the next twenty years is incalculable. Not to mention her eventual sell-off value, and the profit from a possible child with the lordling."

Durux made a hissing sound, more animal than human. Cinder whimpered.

Jatar turned on his heel. "Consider your debt to me paid. The woman is mine. The House of Night is yours. Again. Isn't that what you always wanted?"

Zura slowly faced Cinder with an expression that almost resembled pity. Then she turned and said to Farood, "Let her go. She's Jatar's problem now."

Durux came forward even as the thug reluctantly released her. Cinder tried to whirl and run again, but Durux wrapped her up in his arms. She cringed away from his body pressed against hers. He started dragging her back. "What have you done with my Luathan, clanwoman? I want her back."

"I don't know where she is." It was true. Cinder doubted the smugglers would have kept the girl at the Sand Snake.

"By the time I'm done with you, you'll remember," Durux told her.

"What do you want with me? Of what importance am I to you?"

"I'm not after you, slave," Jatar answered as she was shoved to the front of the chariot. He slapped the reins across the horses' backs. The chariot shot through the city, people leaping out of its way. Cinder couldn't help but watch for Darsam. Surely he was out of prison now and looking for her. He promised he would do anything for her.

They passed the city wall, crossing dozens of orchards fed by the province's ingenious irrigation systems. Cinder stared out into the fields and tried to count the people hurrying to plant the last of the seeds before the rains came in earnest. But the numbers kept slipping away. Clannish and Luathan men and women glanced up at the coming storm and then went back to work, their bodies bent as they prepared for a crop of which they would never taste the fruits.

The chariot shot past the workers' housing, nestled within an orchard. Six long rows of dilapidated buildings with bolted doors and no windows. Cinder dully wished this was the life that now awaited her—endless days of picking fruit and planting crops. Because whatever the slavers had in store for her would be much worse.

Soon, they left the fields and orchards behind and approached a circular wall. Cinder knew if they crossed that wall and Darsam still hadn't come for her, he probably never would. She closed her eyes as she passed beneath its shadow; she swore she could feel the oppressive weight of the stones arching above her.

At that moment the rains came, lashing at her from the side and making her new tattoos sting. Squinting through the water running down her face, Cinder watched as the chariot climbed toward a sprawling mansion. She didn't think it was possible to feel more afraid, but she did. Whatever Jatar meant to do with her would be worse than anything she could imagine.

Jatar stepped past her, into the mansion. Durux took hold of her arm. "May I play with her, Father?"

Father? Jatar is Durux's father? Cinder thought as the water slipped down her skin. She looked at the men and saw nothing to tie them together, from their looks to their temperaments.

Jatar rubbed his forehead. "Why don't you go play with your new man for now—the city watchman. What was his name? Grez?"

Cinder went cold all over.

"Can I kill him?" Durux asked with a sick eagerness.

"Not yet. He hasn't suffered enough."

Durux pivoted, a lightness to his step—like a child about to play with a new toy.

"You're the one who beat up Laz," Cinder choked.

Jatar unwound his dripping cloak and tossed it onto a chair. "Oh, we did much worse than beat him up. His sister is a beautiful girl."

Cinder clenched her fists. "You're just trying to scare me."

He chuckled. "Come along."

Afraid he would call Durux back if she didn't, Cinder trailed after Jatar, leaving puddles of water behind her to mark her path. She wondered if a servant would come along later and wipe it up, or if the water stains would stay a few days as a testament that she had been here.

Jatar led her through the extravagant mansion to the back kitchens. Thirty-eight steps later, he opened a door, releasing a puff of incense, and motioned for her to go ahead of him into what appeared to be a dark cellar. Every muscle in her body clenched. When she hesitated, he gripped her shoulder and shoved her. She stumbled down the stairs, one hand braced against the rough wall to steady herself.

She tried to comfort herself that at least Yula was free. Darsam would make sure she stayed that way.

At the base of the stairs, Jatar gave Cinder one last shove. She barely managed to catch herself from falling. Breaths coming too fast, she found herself in a wine cellar, the shelves of which held more scrolls than wine. It was chilly below, and with her wet clothes, she immediately began to shiver. There was a table in the center littered with paper. All along the perimeter, bowls of crumbling incense burned, the smoke strong enough to sting her eyes and the back of her throat—just like at the Idaran temples. Some people burned incense to keep fairies at bay. Zura had never liked how the smoke had dirtied her walls, so it had never been used at the House of Night.

"I didn't take you for a religious man," Cinder said with a cough.

Jatar chuckled. "I'm rather the opposite of religious." He turned to two guards as they came down to stand at the base of the stairs. "Remind the men at the wall to signal us the moment they see anything."

One guard nodded and turned to go. The second squared himself in front of the stairs. Jatar circled around to the other side of the table and looked over some scrolls. He tossed them aside in frustration before finally looking up at Cinder. "Tell me about Darsam."

She set her jaw. "I'm not telling you anything."

Jatar leaned forward, bracing his weight on the table. "There probably isn't much you can tell me that I don't already know."

She huffed in disbelief. "I doubt that."

He smiled at her. "I know that Lord Bahar has been working for years to underhand the slave and pleasure guilds. I also know that his son only pretends to be a fop. Darsam and his tribesmen friends are really spying out slaves to rescue."

Cinder lifted her chin, trying to be brave even though her she was really shivering and terrified. "If you really knew that, you'd have killed him a long time ago."

"You have no idea how many times I've come close to doing just that," Jatar assured her. "But I've waited, because he was the key."

She tried to quell the desperation rising inside her. "Key to what?"

Jatar squinted at her. "Come closer, so I can see your expressions."

When she didn't move, the guard came forward and dragged her in front of the desk before returning to his post.

Jatar studied her. "At first, we tried to infiltrate Darsam's network. But my spies would always end up dead. Darsam is careful about those he works with—always tribesmen and always infallibly loyal. Until I realized Darsam's weakness. He has a blind spot for those who are helpless. They are the only ones who can come close enough.

"And then you came along. The way he watched you, the way he followed you around, I knew I had to have you as my own. Durux even arranged to bring Darsam running and then have a little trollop push you in front of his chariot, just to prick at the perfect little conscience of his. Zura already owed me enough money, so it wasn't hard to convince her to buy a slave on credit. I even picked out the Luathan girl myself."

"It was all a show?"

"We were certain you'd try to run. Who wouldn't? Zura planted a little tip for Ash about a smuggler who helped slaves. Dutiful mother that she is, she set off immediately, and you even followed her." He chuckled. "When Darsam made a fool of himself at the auction, we knew we had him."

Cinder bowed her head, letting the clumps of her damp hair fall forward to cover her face so Jatar wouldn't see her crestfallen countenance. So he wouldn't know how afraid she was now.

"Even in my wildest schemes," he went on, "I never imagined the fool would fall in love with you."

"He's not in love with me," Cinder said, knowing she had to do what she could to protect Darsam.

Jatar shook his head. "Not what my spy heard from that jail cell you two happened to have shared."

Fire and burning, Jatar did know everything. "What do you want me for?"

125

AMBER ARGYLE

"Weaknesses, Cinder. The goddess has precious few. My men and I have tried to bring her down before, with disastrous results. She is powerful beyond words, well insulated, and has managed to heal herself from what should have been a fatal blow more than once."

Cinder felt the blood draining from her face. "You're going to try to kill the goddess?"

A wicked smile curved up the corners of Jatar's mouth. "No. You are."

She gaped at him and then started laughing, the sound maniacal and desperate. "Me? Have you lost your mind?" Cinder had no more training with a knife than slicing a mango, and none at all with a sword.

"At first, we tried to buy off Nelay's men, but they are loyal to a fault," Jatar explained. "We've tried killing her from afar, but she seems to know we're coming before we do. It was then we learned of her spies, the fairies. Our attacks became more secretive, more complex. We've learned to hide underground and use incense to keep the fairies at bay. We even managed to put a bolt through her once. By the next day, she was airborne, and my men burned.

"Nelay's only weakness is her family, which has proved impenetrable. But you—you can get in. Darsam cares about you. He'll take you where he knows he can keep you safe, back to his palace."

Cinder felt all the blood drain from her face. "So if I help you, what's in it for me?" She wouldn't, but it would be foolish to say so.

Jatar's eyes lit up. "Freedom. For your family. For you."

She was ashamed at how much that offer tempted her. "And if I refuse?"

"Durux has taken an interest in you. He's impossible to live with if he doesn't have his . . . needs met."

"You're as mad as he is."

"My son is not mad. Just evil. But I've found a way to channel him, to leash him. He is quite useful." Cinder shuddered. "When the queen comes to visit," Jatar went on, "you will find a way to give her this." He held up a glass vial filled with a clear liquid. "It's tasteless and odorless. It will make her feel sleepy. And then her heart will stop in her sleep. It will be an easy death."

Cinder shook her head. "I can't." *I can't, I can't, I can't.*

"I thought you might say that." Jatar called out to his guards. The door came open. Storm and Ash walked in, propelled by Durux and a handful of guards.

"Cinder," Ash gasped.

Cinder's breath hitched, panic catching in her throat. Her gaze darted over her mother and grandmother. They didn't appear to be hurt. But Cinder didn't believe that would last long, not with men such as Durux and Jatar.

Durux walked around her family and approached Cinder. She backed away from him but he was fast, his hand snaking out to grab her face. "I will carve furrows in your skin. You will be my masterpiece."

"Leave her alone," Storm cried.

There was a struggle and then ringing silence. Not daring to take her eyes off Durux, to see what had been done to her mother and grandmother, Cinder felt a sob building in her chest.

"Only if she refuses, Son," Jatar said. "If she fails, you can have the older women to play with for as long as you please."

Durux grinned, his teeth flashing.

"I'm not afraid of you, or of him." It was a lie, but it felt like bravery to say it.

Jatar's face was emotionless. "You should be."

Durux licked the tear rolling down Cinder's cheek and released her, his hands out to his sides. "I am a god."

Tears streaming down her face, Cinder moved to stand before her mother and grandmother, who held onto her as if they would never let go. "You promise to leave them alone?"

Ash shuddered, but Storm said, "I don't mind dying, Cinder."

A sob slipped from Cinder's mouth and she barely managed to swallow the others storming behind it. "But Grandmother, he will do so much worse than simply kill you."

Jatar came around the desk to stand before the older woman. "It's all about weaknesses, as I was telling your granddaughter."

"Whatever he wants you to do, don't do it," Storm said to Cinder. "Do you understand me? The only way this ends for any of us is with death."

"Show her, Durux," Jatar said.

Durux backed Storm against the wall and held his blade to her throat. Cinder bolted to stop him, but Jatar pinned her against him. Cinder writhed and kicked in Jatar's arms, wanting to hurt him so badly, to break free and rip Durux's limbs from his body. But Jatar held her as if she were nothing.

"The old ones have tougher spirits, but weaker bodies," Durux said. "You have to be so, so careful if you want to keep them alive." He trailed his knife down Storm's cheek, leaving a livid welt. "So, so careful."

"Stop it!" Cinder sobbed. "I'll do what you want. Just leave them alone!"

Jatar released her and held the vial between them. "Find a way to put it in Nelay's food. Then get out. My men will be watching for you. They'll bring you to your mother and grandmother. As soon as word reaches us that the goddess is dead, I will see you on a boat back to the clanlands myself."

Cinder had to work her mouth a few times before she could make it form any words. "How do I know you'll keep your promise?"

Jatar took her hand. She didn't resist as he set the vial, still warm from his skin, into her palm. "I am a man of my word, Cinder. Darsam will come for you. My men will put up a fight, just enough to make it look good. The queen will be in the city for a few days—at least until her son is well enough to be transferred back to Thanjavar. Find a way to kill her before then, or your family dies."

Before Cinder could answer one way or another, a knock sounded on the door. "Yes?" Jatar called.

The door opened to reveal one of his men. "They've been spotted, sir. Six of them. Just crossing the river. And the other guild leaders are waiting for you."

Jatar's suffocating presence stepped back, and Cinder could breathe again.

"Good. Send them down." The man retreated. Jatar motioned to the guard at the base of the stairs. "Take the older two back to their cells. The girl to Durux's rooms. Dress her in something scandalous—Darsam won't be able to resist coming for her then." Jatar sat behind his desk, even as six men and women wearing fine clothing and the mantles of different guilds— slaver, pleasure, entertainer, even the seamen's guild—slipped downstairs.

The guard took hold of Cinder's arm and hauled her to the top of the stairs. Two more men dragged her family into the dark, stormy night. Cinder latched onto the doorframe to keep from being dragged away. She and her mother and grandmother screamed for each other, reaching for each other, but the men holding them were too strong. The door slammed shut. Ash and Storm were out of her reach. Realizing she might never see them again, Cinder collapsed, her sobs breaking loose.

"Good evening, my friends," Jatar said from below as he addressed the guild leaders facing his desk. "The plan is in place. At my signal, we will begin our coordinated attacks through all the cities of Idara, starting—" The guard shut the cellar door, cutting off any other words he might have said.

The guard hauled Cinder up and took her to another room in the house. An older woman waited there next to a steaming bath. A silk dress with a plunging neckline and a slit up the side hung over the door. Cinder's terrified mind caught up with why they were bathing her and putting her into such fine clothing. But no matter what she wore, she knew Darsam would do whatever it took to save her from becoming Durux's personal toy.

As she was forced into the tub, her mind went back to the words she'd heard earlier. Coordinated attacks on all the cities— this wasn't just about killing the goddess. This was about all of Idara.

CHAPTER ELEVEN

Cinder stood before the open window, blinded to the night by the room lit with dozens of lanterns. Outside, it was raining, great sheets coming down. The spray of water bouncing off the balcony had her damp and shivering. Dressed in cream silk that did little to hide her body, she stood with her arms crossed protectively over her chest. The guard was just off to the side, making sure Cinder stayed where she could easily be seen through the window.

Despite the coolness, she was sweating, drops sliding down the back of her neck. "You know Jatar means you to die," she said softly to the guard, who was barely more than a boy. "When Darsam comes, he'll kill you to free me."

"Not if I kill him first. Durux said you were a companion. So sing. It might help your lover find you easier."

"I don't—"

The guard set his hand on the hilt of his sword. "Sing!"

Cinder swallowed hard, trying to bring up a bit of moisture. But she couldn't think of a song, any song. "I can't think—"

"That song the clanwomen always sing—the one that makes you shiver. Sing that one."

She knew which one he meant. The song about the Southron, a river that cut through most of the clanlands. Cinder began to sing. She knew her voice was nothing special, but the song was. It began with the river feeling the soldiers of Idara cutting through as they invaded. Of the blood that had poisoned its waters, of the bodies it had taken to the sea. Of the ships that had made it to the sea only to go down, bodies and weapons sinking softly into the still depths.

It made Cinder long for all the things she had never seen, but that were part of her, woven through the fabric of her being.

When the song ended, the guard said softly, "What does it mean?"

"It's a lament. The sorrow of the river, a silent witness."

"That's stupid. Rivers can't witness—" His voice cut off in a gurgle and he staggered, trying to turn. A shadowy form shoved him to the ground. Instinctively, Cinder stepped back, but the figure whipped off his cloak, and the lamplight caught his face.

Darsam. Cinder had begun to hope he wouldn't come, that he wouldn't risk himself or his men for her. But if she refused to go with him now, Jatar would have no use for her. Darsam and his men would die. Cinder's family would die.

Darsam settled his cloak over her revealing dress and pulled the hood over her blond hair. "Stay close," he whispered.

He hopped over the balcony, Cinder a step behind him. Neither of them said a word as they stumbled in the dark through the rain, cutting between the rolling hills to avoid being seen. She counted the bruises and welts she earned from the undergrowth—twenty-one by the time they reached the wall.

Darsam took hold of a single rope that dangled down from the top of the wall. "There might be soldiers up there. Let me go first."

She grabbed his arm. "You shouldn't have come back for me."

He pushed a dagger into her hands. "Anyone tries to stop you, stick them with this."

Then he was hauling himself up the rope. Cinder started up right behind him, using the rain-swollen knots someone had tied. She had grasped the seventeenth knot when Darsam reached the top of the wall and motioned for her to wait. After looking around carefully, he leaned down to take her hand.

From the shadows came a rushing sound and movement. Cinder gave a cry of warning. Darsam spun, his sword coming from its sheath with a hiss. There was a brief scuffle. A man screamed as he fell from the top of the wall. He slammed into Cinder, sending her sliding down the rope. The rough fibers burned her palm. When her hands hit the sixteenth knot, her right fingers let go of their grip on the rope, leaving her dangling by her left hand.

"Darsam?" she cried. He couldn't have been the one to have fallen. *That has to be one of Jatar's guards. Has to be. Has to be. Has to be.*

She rotated to grip the rope with her right hand again. She started to slip when a warm palm slapped against the top of her hand. "Cinder!"

After hauling her up to the wall walk and steadying her, Darsam's head whipped around. She followed his gaze and saw lights come on in the guard house. He pulled up the rope, took two steps to the other side of the wall, and threw the rope down. "You first. Hurry," he told Cinder.

Heart pounding with fear at her near fall, she looked down to see shadows moving in the stillness. "There's something down there."

"My men."

"Darsam." The voice cracked like a teenage boy's. "Quit dancing with the lady and let's go!"

"My strings are wet," another man complained. Cinder thought she recognized Ashar's voice. "Not even sure if the blasted crossbow will shoot."

Knowing Jatar didn't need these men alive—except for Darsam—gave Cinder the courage to swing her leg over the wall. She focused on the rope, trying to forget about the fall to the bottom. The sound of a bolt firing and a distant cry of pain alerted her to the guards who were coming.

"Oh, good, they still work," said the boy's voice. Cinder looked down. In the darkness, all she could see were moving shadows. "Jump," the boy called to her.

Her fingers clenched the knot. She wondered what number it was. "I can't see anything."

"I'm right under you. Jump!" repeated the boy.

Darsam stepped on Cinder's hand. She tried to gauge the distance in the dark, but then she heard hacking sounds.

"Cinder, they're cutting the rope!"

She closed her eyes and let go. Arms windmilling, she fell through the air. She landed on what she thought was a horse's rump, which made the animal lunge forward. Cinder toppled to the muddy ground with her skirt tangled around her legs. She pushed to her feet. Something bumped into her, so she reached out. Fur and leather. A horse.

"Get on." It was definitely Ashar's voice.

"I don't know how to ride," she admitted.

"Hang on and let your legs absorb the shock," Darsam said from above her. Somehow he'd gotten down from the rope and mounted a horse, while she'd barely made it to her feet. Her fumbling hands finally found the stirrup, and she managed to climb into the saddle.

The animal bolted toward the blackness, and it was all Cinder could do to stay in the saddle. As they cut across country on a dirt road that wove through the orchards, mud flung up behind them and pelted their backs. Jatar's men gave chase. They were gaining on them.

"Denar!" Darsam said.

Behind them, a wall of multicolored flames roared up—it had to be luminash—bringing the pursuers' horses up short. In the light of those flames, Cinder saw Jatar among the men. He pointed to the person riding on the other side of her, a boy of around thirteen. "There he is! Bring him down!"

A dozen men aimed their crossbows at the boy, who had to be Denar, the wielder of the luminash. A dozen bolts shot toward him. A blast of hot wind rose up from nowhere, nearly forcing Cinder from her saddle. When she looked back, Denar seemed unhurt, and the archers were nearly out of range. The wall of flames continued to burn bright and hot, preventing Jatar and his men from following.

Cinder turned in time to see lights reflecting off the ground in front of them. She didn't understand what she was seeing until she heard the rushing sound and realized it was the river reflecting the firelight.

"Denar, you all right?" asked Darsam.

"Fine," the boy said lightly.

Darsam maneuvered his horse in front of Cinder's. "We have to ford the river. If we can reach the other side, we can disappear into the night."

"I can't—I can't swim," Cinder protested. Fire and burning, she was going to die tonight. Maybe that was better. She couldn't betray Darsam if she died.

He pulled his mount around. "Just hold on," he told her. "Let your horse do the swimming." The animals in front stepped hesitantly into the dark water, and at the urging of their riders, waded deeper. Darsam and Cinder followed, and suddenly she could feel her horse swimming beneath her—the movements surprisingly graceful and smooth. Two more of Darsam's men brought up the rear.

Cinder winced as a wave splashed over her legs. "What about crocodiles . . . and snakes?"

No one answered, but she noticed Darsam and his men watching the water, swords out. Leaning low over her horse's neck, she breathed in the animal's wet-dusty smell, trying to pretend she was in the House of Night's stables instead of in the middle of a reptile-infested river with slavers on her tail.

Suddenly, the light was gone. Cinder looked back to see only a smoldering line of red where ten-foot flames had been. Something splashed upriver. She turned to see a riderless horse. Where was Denar?

Something hit Cinder's leg, and her horse lunged forward. Hoping she was right and it was Denar and not a crocodile, she reached out. At the touch of cloth under her fingers, she fumbled to grasp the boy's arms and pull him up. He wasn't as heavy or as large as she'd first thought. With the help of the current, she managed to get his chest onto her saddle. Pinning him with her elbow, she felt him over, trying to figure out what was wrong. A quarrel stuck out of his right shoulder. *He must have been hit by the first volley.* But he hadn't even cried out, just kept riding.

Guilt surged through Cinder. Denar came to help free her. And now he'd been shot.

Her horse calmed a little and started swimming after the others. The river kept trying to pull Denar from Cinder's arms, but she strained to hold on. When her mount caught purchase on the muddy bank, the boy started slipping from Cinder's grip.

Bracing herself, she called out to Darsam, "Help!"

The other riders turned toward her. "Denar!" one of the men cried.

"I told you we shouldn't have let him come," Ashar said.

"His mother is going to kill us," said another.

Darsam hoisted Denar onto his saddle. "There was no leaving him behind, and you all know it." He looked back at Cinder. "It's not far to the city. But you have to keep up."

She nodded. "I will."

Then the horses were thundering toward the city gleaming white and gold in the distance.

CHAPTER TWELVE

Cinder followed Darsam as he held Denar in his arms and shouldered his way into the palace. Behind him scrambled his men and a handful of city and palace guards. In the palace lights, she recognized a limping Ashar. He and another man broke off from the group in search of the healer. Darsam moved from a receiving area to a room just past the back staircase. While his men spread out around him, he set Denar down on the table. The gangly youth of perhaps thirteen, with peach fuzz on his upper lip, was conscious now. He gritted his teeth against the pain and gasped.

It is my fault, my fault, my fault, Cinder thought.

Denar's gaze locked on her. "Ah, now I see why you insisted we save her."

"I told you to stay back," Darsam growled. He was covered in the boy's blood.

"Only because you were afraid that once she saw me, she'd forget all about you."

Cinder's mouth fell open. "What?"

Darsam ripped off the boy's robe. "Denar is the biggest flirt you'll ever meet—but he's harmless. Mostly."

Despite the fact that his lips were turning a lurid purple, Denar winked at her. Cinder studied his wound. The bolt hadn't passed all the way through—the feathered end still bristled from his back. She didn't know much about wounds or healing, but she didn't think this was the sort of thing one survived.

Denar had risked his life to save her, and now he was dying. "How can you be so relaxed about it?" she asked him.

The boy coughed, blood running down his cheek. His entire mouth was red with it. "My mother won't let me die."

"The rest of you, go," Darsam said to his men as he packed the wound with cloth. "If his mother doesn't know already, she will soon. No need to be here when she comes."

"His mother?" Cinder said in confusion.

"The goddess, Queen Nelay," Darsam replied.

She gasped softly. The boy's mother was the goddess that Cinder was supposed to kill.

"She has a bit of a temper," the boy managed. Bloody foam sprayed from his mouth as he coughed.

"The healer is coming," Ashar said as he entered the room, his limp more pronounced now. "Why should you be the one to face her?" He directed the question to Darsam.

Darsam frowned. "I was the one who needed your help, so I will take responsibility." He nodded toward Cinder. "Take her with you."

Ashar started toward her. "I'm not going anywhere," she exclaimed, moving away from him.

A woman in healer's robes and messy hair hurried into the room. "May the fire protect us," she gasped. She pushed Darsam out of the way. "Out, the lot of you!"

Darsam backed toward the door, his eyes not leaving the prince. "His mother is the Goddess of Fire," Darsam told Cinder. "And she has a temper like wildfire. Once she finds out I allowed her son to come with us on this mission, she may very well kill me."

This was why Jatar had followed Cinder after she'd left the mansion. Why he had ordered his men to shoot at the prince and no one else. To lure in the goddess. *My fault, my fault, my fault.*

"You needed me, Darsam," the boy said, his skin gray. "And I didn't give you much of a choice."

The healer shot them an exasperated look. "Out! All of you!"

Darsam took hold of Cinder's arm and guided her out. He pulled her fifteen steps down the corridor and into another room. Cushions surrounded a low table. A utilitarian bed rested against one corner. It was his room, she realized with a start as he shut the door behind him.

He pulled her back to arms' length and looked her up and down. Under his cloak, she still wore the scandalous dress from Jatar, which was soaking wet from the rain and the river. Mud was mixed in there too. And blood. Uncomfortable with Darsam's scrutiny, Cinder crossed her arms over her breasts, but he was already moving to a table. He picked up a bucket and dumped water into a basin.

He laid out soap and a wash rag and asked, "Did he hurt you?"

Cinder couldn't meet Darsam's gaze, afraid he would see the treachery there. But she had to follow through with Jatar's plan and kill the queen. Otherwise, Durux would torture and kill Cinder's mother and grandmother. "No. He didn't hurt me," she answered after several seconds.

Obviously relieved, Darsam said, "Wash up. I'm going to go find you some clothes." He left the room.

Cinder started to strip down but paused when she felt the vial sewed into the bosom of the dress. She pulled it out and held it up to the light. Her fingers were dirty and bloody, but they would wash clean. If she did this, her soul would forever be stained.

I don't have a choice. She hid the vial behind the basin. She yanked off the dress, not caring when the silk ripped, then balled up the gown and threw it into a corner. Next, she wet a washcloth and did the best she could to clean up. Touching the welts on her legs brought a hiss from her lips.

Cinder was debating whether to try to clean her hair when Darsam called her name. Her gaze darted to where she'd hidden the vial, and she realized what a poor job she'd done of it. "Don't come in!"

"I've brought clothes."

She went to the door and stuck out her bare arm. He pushed something into her grip and said, "They're my sister's. I think they should fit."

Cinder slipped on the trousers and robe, noticing the exceptional craftsmanship. She tucked the vial into the breast wrap, checked to make sure it wouldn't be noticed from the outside, and opened the door. "Is Denar really the prince?" she asked.

Holding a bucket of water, Darsam stepped inside and shut the door behind him. "Yes. He is Nelay's son."

Cinder didn't know where to put her hands. "What will she do?"

Darsam dumped her used water out the window and poured some fresh for himself. "You don't need to worry. You'll never go back to slavery again. We'll hide you in the palace until it's safe to sneak you out of the city."

Why did he have to be so kind? So perfect? "And go where?"

He stripped off his bloody robes, revealing broad, defined muscles. He pushed his red hands into the water, took the soap, and began to lather up the same cloth Cinder had used. "I imagine you want to go back to the clanlands. They're your people, regardless of whether or not you were born an Idaran."

Even now, he would ask nothing of her. She wished he would. Wished he would prove himself to be something less. "Why did you come for me?" she asked him. "Why did you risk so much?"

"I couldn't just leave you with Durux. I know what kind of monster he is." Darsam rinsed the cloth out and began wiping the soap from his body. "I made the rest of them stay behind—I wouldn't risk their lives. Just my own. And I still managed to get Denar shot."

She watched as Darsam ducked his head in the water and soaped up his hair. He was a lord's son. A smuggler. He could be and have anything he wanted, and yet he'd given up any chance at a normal, long life in order to help slaves. Cinder felt a rush of affection for this man who was so kind and good and gentle.

"So you would have done the same for any other slave?" she asked him.

He wrung the water from his hair and turned to face her, droplets slipping down his skin. His dark eyes met her silver ones. She saw it in his gaze—a tenderness. "I told you, I would do anything for you."

Darsam cared about her—maybe he was even in love with her. In all the world, she didn't think she'd ever find his equal. But he would never be hers, because she had to kill his aunt to save her own mother and grandmother.

Cinder stepped forward, took Darsam's face in her hands, and kissed him. He responded immediately, wrapping his arms around her and pulling her close. The kiss was tender and bitter-sweet, his lips soft and giving. But there was a trace of heat against her frozen skin. His hands trembled as he touched her hair.

What if she'd been wrong about him? She *wanted* to be wrong about him. She knew how to find out. She deepened the kiss. Her hands moved to the tie of his robes, but he rested his hands on her, gently holding her in place. "Cinder, why are you crying?"

Surprised, she reached up and touched her cheek.

"I know you're upset," Darsam said quietly. "I know you're frightened. But I've told you before, you don't have to *give* me anything. You don't owe me anything. If something is going to happen between us, I want it to be because you care about me as much as I care about you. Not because you feel you have to."

He put a little distance between them. Without him to hold her up, Cinder collapsed in on herself, holding her arms and sobbing. Immediately, Darsam moved close again and took her into his arms. "What is it? What's wrong?"

How could she tell him that she wanted something more between them? Wanted it just as much as she'd ever wanted to be free? But she would never have him because she had to betray him.

There was a rushing sound, like the roar of wildfire. Darsam pulled back. "Stay here," he ordered. He grabbed a clean robe from a chest, jerked open his door, and rushed down the hall. Wiping her eyes, Cinder followed right behind him and was suddenly inundated with the smell of baked sand. Inside the sickroom, a woman stood over the prince, wings of fire spreading from her back and filling the whole space with a dangerous heat.

She looked up as they came in, flames dancing in her eyes. "What have you done to my son?"

143

CHAPTER THIRTEEN

Darsam noticed Cinder as she caught up to him. He pushed her behind him, then held out his free hand toward the queen. "You know how Denar is. He takes after his parents."

"He's a thirteen-year-old boy!" Nelay shot back.

"He saved our lives," Darsam said softly, "when he created the fire that blocked the slavers."

The queen's wings expanded. "How dare you put him at risk? He—"

Denar rested a hand on her arm. "Mother, you're going to burn down the palace, and our aunt and uncle and all our cousins with it."

"I only plan to burn *him* down." Nelay stabbed her finger in Darsam's direction.

"You will do no such thing!" a voice cried. A woman came into the room, her hair in a messy braid. She wore a loose robe over her sleeping clothes and was obviously pregnant. She planted herself in front of Darsam. "Nelay, Darsam is my stepson. *Your* nephew."

"Maran . . ." Nelay growled.

Fire and burning, Cinder thought *her* family was complicated. At least she wasn't related to a queen who also happened to be a goddess. Cinder was drenched in sweat, her skin near to blistering.

Another man entered the room and he looked so like Darsam he could only be his father. Ignoring the cluster of people at the door, and the overwhelming heat, he went straight to the bed and asked, "How are you, boy?"

Nelay's gaze turned to her son. "Mother," he gasped, and Cinder could see him struggling to breathe. He was dying, she realized. A rush of shame made her stagger back.

The goddess's fire died out as if it had never been. "Tix, get me the petal!" she ordered.

Five seconds later, a spider crawled across the ceiling and dropped a silk-covered bundle. The queen stretched out her hand and caught it, then tore away the spider silk to reveal a white petal with a burgundy-and-yellow center. She pushed the petal toward her son's mouth.

Denar turned away. "Only if you promise not to hurt them—any of them."

Nelay hesitated. "But they deserve to be punished!"

He took her hand, wrapping it in his long, awkward fingers. "That's the fairy in you talking."

She softened a fraction. "Very well, I swear not to harm any of them."

He opened his mouth obediently, and she pushed the flower onto his tongue. Immediately, his eyes slipped closed, his body relaxing against the pain. His skin lost the gray hue, while his breathing went from labored to easy in the space of a few inhales.

Nelay bent forward, her face all gentleness now, and pressed her lips to his forehead. "Sleep well, my Denar."

Then she lifted stern eyes to the rest of them. "You have some explaining to do."

They followed the queen into the corridor, through a door, and then up a long series of seemingly neverending steps. While they climbed, Darsam introduced Cinder his father—a man who looked remarkably like his son, right down to the square jaw and wavy hair. And his stepmother, Maran, a woman with a tranquil, wise presence. Studying her rounded belly, Cinder wondered how many siblings Darsam had. She felt ashamed she'd never thought to ask.

A total of 502 steps took her to the top of one of the high towers. Open to the elements, the spot was safer if the queen decided to turn into flames. It was raining again, the drops hissing and steaming if they came anywhere near the queen. The cool, damp breeze felt wonderful against Cinder's skin as she took a cup from a tray a servant had brought, hoping to steel her resolve.

And she realized that her entire life, she had thought of her life as a "before" and "after." She'd been living in the "before" while working toward the "after." After she got a job. After she freed her family. After they left Idara for good. But now, everything had changed. Every beat of her heart, every intake of breath brought her closer to the moment when everything would change into a different after—one she would never truly survive, even if she did manage to escape with her life.

Darsam told the story of how Cinder's freedom was stolen from her. Of how he'd saved her from Jatar's compound. He made her sound better, stronger, than she really was. Nelay listened, her arms folded over her chest, her gaze fixed to the north. Cinder faced out over the sleeping city, counting the beats of her heart as the moments of "before" dwindled down to nearly nothing.

When Darsam finished, Nelay took a deep breath and faced Cinder. "You saved him from the river. For that, I thank you."

Cinder stared at this woman, the enemy of her people. The queen of the land that had held her family in slavery for decades. If Cinder failed, her mother and grandmother's blood would spill.

Without answering, Cinder set down her now empty cup. Her back to the others, she held the vial in her fis as she stared at the remaining cups. If the queen found out, she would turn her to ash with barely a thought. If Cinder succeeded, she would never see Darsam again.

"Cinder?" he said softly. "Are you well?"

She glanced over her shoulder to where he sat with his legs folded and his wrists resting on his knees, his brow creased with concern. Something hitched within her. Whatever she felt for him, he didn't deserve her betrayal. But what choice did she have?

"I'm just worried about my mother and grandmother." She had to choose. Save one—Darsam. Or save two—her mother and grandmother. Cinder couldn't live with herself if she let her family fall into Durux's hands.

Before she could change her mind, she turned her back to Darsam and emptied the vial into the orray. She let the last few drops drip, drip, drip into the cup, the liquid rippling with poison. Hands shaking, she went about handing the drinks out to Darsam and his stepmother and father. They were good people— the kind of people who banished slavery. Cinder was betraying them too.

Averting her gaze in shame, she held out the cup for the queen. Heat radiating from her skin, the woman stretched to take the cup—the seconds of "before" finished—and Cinder saw the "after." The goddess would grow tired and retire to her rooms. She would not wake again, not ever. Cinder would run back to the slavers. Durux had promised he would free her and her mother and grandmother.

And perhaps he would.

But it wouldn't end there. His insurgents would rise up and slaughter all the tribesmen in power, including the boy who'd nearly died trying to save Cinder. Including Darsam and his entire family. The slavers and brothels would reopen. More slaves would be bought and sold. More girls like Storm and Yula would be wrenched away from their families. More children would be born into the same position as their mothers. And Idara would go back to conquering every nation in the world and enslaving their people.

If Cinder did this, she was no better than a slaver herself. She couldn't live with this "after." Her breath hitching, she tipped the edge of the cup and let the orray dribble onto the stone. A different "after" opened up before her, and she swore she could feel the beats of her heart ticking down to her own death.

"What are you doing?" the queen gasped as the liquid danced and sizzled at her feet.

Staggering, Cinder turned her back on everyone and went to stand at the edge of the tower. She looked out over the city and wondered where her family was—how much longer until the beats of their heart stilled. Grief tore through her, and she almost wished she could take it back. But it was too late now.

"I cannot kill you, Goddess," she managed to choke out.

Sharp inhales came from all around, and Cinder felt a flare of heat burning into her back, so hot she wondered if her hair would catch fire. She had to close her eyes at the sudden bright light. The wind picked up, rain stinging her skin. Thunder rumbled in the distance.

"Jatar has my mother and grandmother," Cinder explained. "If I kill you, they go free. If not, he will give them to Durux to torture and kill." She said the last bit for Darsam's sake, so he would understand why she had even considered it.

"The magic is trying to force you to be something you're not," Maran said to the queen. "Fight it, Nelay,"

Cinder wiped her tears and slowly turned to face the goddess. The whole tower was steaming, the wind whipping the vapors away as soon as they formed. Lightning flashed. Everyone else had taken shelter behind a column from the blistering heat. Cinder lifted her arm to protect her eyes. "But that is not all," she continued. "After you are dead, he plans to stage a coup. Coordinated attacks throughout Idara will kill all the tribesmen lords and put the old lords back in their places."

"Why are you telling me this?" Nelay's fists were clenched, her body rigid, as if she were trying to keep back the fire by force of will.

The hair on Cinder's arms withered, curling in on itself. She had a feeling she might already be unconscious if not for the cool rain lashing against her skin. "Because you aren't my enemy. Slavery is. And one day, you will rid Idara of slavery all together, so that no man, woman, or child shall ever have to endure as my family has endured."

Flames skipped across the goddess's skin in time to the lightning crashing down around the tower. "The slavers hurt my son to maneuver me into a position so that you could kill me," she said. Flames licked across the floor toward Cinder.

Darsam suddenly stepped before her, his arm raised to shield himself from the heat. "Remember what else she did, Nelay! She saved Denar—she pulled him from the river. And she risked her family's lives to warn us! Focus on that."

The queen trembled with heat, her jaw tight, her skin translucent. Flames licked through her veins, and sparks glinted in her eyes.

"You promised Denar you wouldn't hurt any of us," Darsam reminded her.

The flames advanced no farther, but the heat didn't abate. Cinder was starting to feel sick with it.

Maran stepped up in front of her son. "Nelay Arel Mandana ShaBejan, you let the fairy take you once, and you've never forgiven yourself for it. Will you do so again?"

With a piercing scream, Nelay turned away from them. Fire jettisoned out from her body, shooting harmlessly out over the palace. Night turned to day. Just as suddenly, everything went dark. There was only the pounding of the rain, the hiss of the steam, and the panting of the queen.

Footsteps moved toward Nelay. "Can you manage a little light?" Maran asked her gently.

A gleaming blue nimbus appeared in the center of the tower, revealing Nelay crumpled to the floor, Maran beside her with her arms on the queen's shoulders. The columns around them had turned black.

Nelay dragged a hand through her hair. "I'm sorry."

"You beat it back," Maran said. "That's what matters."

The queen slowly pushed herself to her feet and turned to face Cinder. The otherworldly aura was gone, leaving behind a woman who seemed tired. "We goddesses always have to fight to keep the fairy from taking over. It's especially hard for me as a fire goddess, which comes with all the passion and impulsivity of summer, you see."

Cinder blinked—one, two, three times. It almost sounded like the goddess had just apologized to her. Not sure how to react, Cinder simply nodded.

It seemed to be enough, for Nelay looked away. "Jatar must be dealt with. Tix!"

A blur appeared at Nelay's side, and then an enormous spider landed on her shoulder. "How did your spies not know about this threat?"

The spider made a whispery, scratchy sound with a structure that made it almost sound like a language. "I want them all found," Nelay said with fervor. "Everyone who had any part of this. Jatar first. I will burn him and all his men to the ground."

"No!" Cinder pushed in front of Darsam. "My mother and grandmother are mixed in with him. As well as dozens and dozens of slaves. If you burn Jatar and his men, you kill them too!"

When the goddess met her gaze, Cinder felt as if the heat would scorch her from the inside out. "They are already dead," Nelay declared. "As soon as you poured out the poison, Jatar would have killed them."

Cinder felt herself crumpling from the inside out. "But there's no way Jatar could know yet."

"Do you honestly think he failed to notice my display earlier?"

"A mother can lose her temper when her son is nearly murdered," Maran said quietly.

Darsam stepped up beside Cinder. "How was he supposed to find out that the queen was dead?"

Cinder shook her head. "All I know is I was supposed to sneak out after it was done. He said he'd find me."

"There's no way Jatar could know. We're the only ones on this tower." Bahar went to the forgotten tray and picked up a cup of orray. "Here, drink it. He will have men watching the palace."

Nelay eyed the cup and then shot a distrustful look at Cinder, who shifted uncomfortably and said, "I poured out the poisoned one."

The goddess tipped this cup and drank the liquid, then made a face. "Uck. Still making it too strong."

Bahar smiled, and something seemed to pass between them. "A strong drink for strong warriors," he said.

Nelay took another drink. "If what you say is true, Cinder, I'll have to go into hiding. Otherwise, Jatar will kill your mother and grandmother when he learns we've betrayed him."

"My men and I could sneak in," Darsam said. He looked at Cinder. "If you could just manage to get them out of his reach for a little while."

"I can try," she replied.

They made plans into the night. Even with the orray, Cinder fell asleep halfway through the preparations. When she woke, she was lying on the cushions in a library, a blanket thrown over her shoulders. It was still the middle of the night, so she had slept for an hour or two at most.

She started when she saw the goddess crouching before her. Nelay looked so normal—curvy, with dark hair and eyes. Intricate, colorful tattoos along the sides of her scalp spilled onto her cheeks. Cunning sparked in her eyes.

"It's really very clever, you know."

Six words that made no sense. "Goddess?"

"Using my child to maneuver me into a position of weakness. Very clever indeed. I might just have to use it myself. But it will take years and careful planning. A warrior must be found. One with the strength to survive such a formidable place."

"I'm not sure I understand."

Nelay shook herself. "It is of no importance at present. I have gifts for you." She held out her palm, revealing an enormous, furry spider. Cinder gasped and scrambled back. The queen watched her impassively. "It is not what it appears."

Cinder held a hand over her racing heart for five beats and then sucked in a breath. "It's a fairy?" Idarans were both fascinated and terrified of them. She wasn't sure what to think of the fairies—her grandmother had always stubbornly insisted they weren't real. Cinder figured if there were fairy queens, there must be fairies.

Nelay held the spider close and stroked its back. "Her name is Tix, and she is the master of my spies. Wherever this Jatar is, he's evaded her notice. Take her with you. When you have found his lair, let her go."

Cinder steeled herself and took the spider. It stared up at her, far too much intelligence in its eight eyes. "And if it's a place even a fairy can't escape from?"

"Then kill her. She will reincarnate into the body of another spider and find me."

Cinder shuddered. "Am I just supposed to put it in my robes or something?"

As if offended, the spider made a scritchity noise and scurried up Cinder's arm, then tucked itself into the fold at the front of her robes. She had to stop herself from squealing and smashing the spider flat. "Just hold still," she pleaded. "I don't think I can stand it if you move."

In answer, the spider held perfectly still and stared at Cinder with baleful eyes.

With a smile touching the corners of her mouth, Nelay held out her other hand. Inside it was a small snake with tan skin and a black tongue. Cinder scrambled back. "A cobra!"

"Her name is Siseth. She will defend you if need be."

A fairy, obviously. But it didn't look like a fairy. It looked like a deadly snake. Cinder held out her hand and shivered as the snake slithered under her sleeve and wound around her upper arm.

Nelay turned without a word and left.

Darsam strode toward Cinder, his shoulders stiff. "It's time for you to go," he told her.

The night's shadows seemed to deepen, becoming a thing alive. And that thing was hungry and full of teeth. "Darsam—"

"Not here, Cinder. Come with me."

They moved down the spiraling stairs. At another door, he pulled her inside.

She needed to apologize, to try to explain. But what came out of her mouth was "How is Denar?"

"The elice blossom will heal him." Darsam nodded to a wall bristling with weapons. "What do you need?"

Cinder sighed. "I lost my tension wrench and rake pin. Any chance you could get me another?" He opened a drawer and handed her a full set of pins. Cinder stuck them in her breast wrap for safekeeping. "What else?"

She surveyed the weapons, resisting the urge to count them. "I don't know how to handle anything else." She dropped her head. "Darsam, I'm sorry. Sorry I didn't tell you sooner."

"You should have." His voice was hard. "I thought you trusted me."

She shuffled her feet. "Durux tortured that watchmen—Grez. He held a knife to my grandmother's face. Jatar knew everything about you. Knew everything about me. And Durux—" A wave of terror tore through Cinder. "I'm gambling my family's lives to save yours. I thought I was going to die for telling the truth."

"Promise me that next time, you'll trust me." Darsam's voice was softer now.

She nodded.

"I'm sorry I was angry," he said. "That wasn't fair."

She nodded again.

He pulled down a dagger, hesitated, and put it back. Then he grabbed two small knives, no longer than his hand, and pushed them into Cinder's palms. Feeling the weight of them, solid and steady, she said, "I don't know how to use these."

Darsam circled her fingers around the hilts. "Hold it like this and thrust or slash." She stared at the knife in her shaking hand. He gripped her wrist. "A fight isn't won with a blade, Cinder. It's won here, in your mind." He touched her temple. "You hold nothing back and you don't stop."

She met his gaze. "What if I can't win?"

"Dying isn't something to fear—it comes to us all. If it comes to you, you will meet it knowing you did the right thing." His steadiness settled the chaotic tumbling inside her. "Thank you for not lying to me, for not telling me it's going to be all right." She pushed the knives back into his hands. "Jatar will suspect me when he finds these."

Darsam gave a frustrated sigh and put the knives back on the shelf. Then he stepped closer and pressed a kiss to her brow. "I'm coming for you. Just as fast as I can. Hold out until then."

Cinder wrapped her arms around him, and he led her to a dark bedroom. "Wait until I'm gone and sneak out the window. There are guards at the gate. They'll let you pass."

He squeezed her hand and slipped out the door. Grateful the rain had stopped for now, she waited a dozen heartbeats before sliding the window open and stepping out onto the flagstones. Moving around the puddles, she slipped past the darkened windows. Cinder saw no one but swore she could feel eyes on her.

At the gates, the guards looked up. "What are you doing out this late, miss?" one of them asked.

"I need to head home before my parents catch me gone," Cinder said. It was the story Darsam had instructed her to tell.

"One of Darsam's girls," muttered the other guard.

Exactly how many girls sneak out of here in the middle of the night? she wondered.

The guard on the left pursed his lips in disapproval. "There are thieves and thugs roaming the streets of late."

"I am far more afraid of my father than any thief," Cinder replied. "Please let me pass."

Begrudgingly, the guards unlocked the gate and let her through. She stepped into the heart of the city, all pristine buildings and shops. Jatar had not told her where to go, just that he would find her. Instinctively she headed towards the bowels of the city, toward the tanning district, where she'd first met Durux inside a building lined with desperation and hopelessness.

Just before Cinder moved out of sight of the palace, she turned back and studied its dark towers, wondering if Darsam was watching her. She was tempted to wave a final goodbye, but then shook herself at the ridiculousness of the idea. He'd promised to follow her to Jatar's lair, so he was probably close. On a rooftop, perhaps. Or shadowing her from one street to the next.

Cinder hurried along. She'd counted 599 steps when a door squeaked open to her right. A man stood in the shadows of some kind of shop. He leaned forward just enough for the moonlight to illuminate his large ears. Durux. She took an automatic step back. The breeze took that moment to blow up from the west, bringing with it the stench of the tanneries.

She steeled herself, promising she would kill him if she had to. He stayed in sight just long enough for her to get a good look at him before disappearing back inside. She swallowed hard, every instinct demanding she turn and flee. She reached out and brushed her fingers at the bulge in her robes and felt a little reassurance at the pressure of the snake around her arm. Reminding herself that she wasn't alone, she stepped inside the building. Ahead of her, Durux was rapidly disappearing down a long corridor.

Cinder cast a glance back at the street, hoping Darsam wasn't far behind. That this would be over soon. But turning back revealed the man was already nearly out of sight.

Tapping her fingers to her thumb to soothe herself, Cinder hurried after him. At the back of the building was a crooked door. She pushed through it into a narrow alley. Durux's shoulders were hunched as he slipped into a derelict building. Coming up behind him, she stared into the windows housing jagged bits of glass. Beams had fallen in, crisscrossing the interior like an orb weaver's trap.

"Is Darsam far?" she asked the spider—Tix, she thought her name was.

The spider said something in a sticky voice Cinder didn't understand.

"I don't speak spider." In response, the spider poked her with one of her spindly legs, leaving behind an itchy spot.

Resisting the urge to scratch at it, Cinder stepped into the shadows. She could feel hard bits of broken glass and the hollow cracking of dead bugs under her feet. She ducked under a beam, wondering where Durux had gone.

"Hello?" she called out. There was no answer. Looking back and forth, she thought she caught a bit of light off to one side and started for it. She hadn't taken five steps when the floor gave out beneath her. She fell through smoke and shadows.

CHAPTER
FOURTEEN

Cinder landed in a heap. Above her, a trapdoor snapped shut, leaving her alone in the dark. She lay on the ground and tried to regain her bearings. She held her hands out to feel the walls around her, but there was nothing. Suddenly, she was a little girl again, shoved in the cellar. Alone for days in the dark.

Counting to calm herself, she reminded herself she wasn't a child anymore. And she certainly wasn't helpless. She reached for the spider and felt an unmoving lump in her shirt. She shifted her focus to the snake and realized she no longer felt its reassuring grip around her arm.

On her hands and knees, Cinder scrabbled around until she felt something cold and smooth. She picked it up, but it was limp and unmoving. "I think Siseth is dead."

She waited for Tix to poke her again, but the spider was as unmoving as the snake. Cinder started at the sound of rushing footsteps and reminded herself to remain calm. After all, she wanted to be taken to Jatar. Not knowing what else to do, she shoved the snake into her robes with the spider. Arms snatched her, hauled her up, and searched her. Then she was led down a narrow tunnel.

"Welcome, little clanwoman." The voice belonged to Durux.

Cinder shuddered, unable to see anything in the darkness. It was hard to breathe through the smoke, which left an almost sweet taste in the back of her throat. *Incense*, she realized. Idarans used it to keep fairies away. Judging by the limp bodies of the fairies tucked into her robe, it worked.

She counted 168 steps before a door appeared. Light lined the seams, smoke curling away from the edges. Cinder could make out pickaxes and buckets of ore lining the tunnels. A guard hauled open the door, and Durux pulled her inside. She blinked at the sudden light and instant change of her surroundings.

It was a lavish room of red and gold, the rough-hewn walls almost completely covered in beautiful tapestries. Pacing before a long table, Jatar squinted suspiciously at her through hooded eyes. "Is the goddess dead?"

Cinder steeled herself. "Yes."

"And the fire show earlier?"

"Her son nearly died. She was angry."

Jatar's eyes flicked a question to Durux. "We've been unable to confirm anything, save the goddess retired to a room."

Jatar nodded. "Find out for certain."

"And if our spy is discovered?" Durux asked.

"Then our spy is no more use to us."

Durux pivoted and left without another word. The guard gave Cinder a warning glance and shut the door behind him.

"You'll forgive me if I'm skeptical," Jatar said. "It's only been a few hours since I released you."

Cinder shrugged like she didn't care. "Where are Ash and Storm?"

"Alive. For the moment."

She wet her lips. "You promised to let us go."

"Once it has been confirmed that the queen is dead."

Cinder's gaze shifted to the bowls of incense lining the room, just like in the cellar earlier. She bit the inside of her cheek. The goddess had said to kill the spider, but Cinder didn't know how to get her out of her robes without alerting Jatar to the fairies' presence. "Can I see my family?"

"No," replied Jatar.

She turned away from him, pretending to wipe her eyes. With her other hand, she grasped the spider fairy. It was the size of her hand and covered with spindly hair. Suppressing a shudder, she pulled the creature free. It looked at her with a hazy yet eager expression.

Cinder dropped the spider and crushed its head. It squirmed, the limbs scrabbling. She pushed harder, shuddering when something gave with a pop. The spider's limbs curled up just as Cinder felt a presence behind her.

"What are you doing?"

For a big man, Jatar could move with surprising stealth. Cinder whirled around. "Nothing. I—" She froze when she saw the knife gleaming in his hand.

"You didn't betray me to them, did you, Cinder?"

She opened her mouth, but her tongue couldn't seem to grasp any of the words her lungs tried to force through it. She managed to shake her head.

"Because the goddess is blind to anything underground. And the incense makes both her and the fairies weak. That, along with her family, is the only weakness I have ever been able to discover. The only weaknesses I have ever been able to exploit. She won't be able to find you here. You and your grandmother and your mother are all alone, helpless against me."

Cinder had to delay him as long as possible. Give Darsam time to reach her. "I gave her the poison."

Jatar grabbed her throat and roughly pushed her against the wall. "Zura has told me all about you, little companion. About how many dozens of men bid for you." He stepped closer and said in her ear. "Durux can have you for free."

She squirmed, trying to get the snake to slide to the back of her robes before Jatar felt it. Beside her, the door opened. "The goddess is dead," Durux reported.

Jatar released Cinder. "It's confirmed?"

Durux nodded.

Jatar lifted his chin, excitement flashing across his eyes. "Good. Move the men into place. Give the signal for the other cities. Tonight we take back what is ours."

He started toward the door, having completely forgotten Cinder. "Wait," she exclaimed. "What about my family? You promised to let us go!"

He paused long enough to glance back at her. "When I see the queen's body for myself, little clanwoman. Then and only then."

The door slammed in her face, and she heard the lock turn. She knew what happened next. Jatar and his forces would move on the palace. When they found the Immortals prepared for them and the goddess very much alive, they would retreat. Any who survived would be heading back to this hideout. Back to Cinder's mother and grandmother.

She didn't know how long it would take Darsam to find her. How long until Jatar realized she had lied. Cinder pulled her tools from her breast wrap, bent before the lock, and inserted her tension wrench and rake pin. More difficult than the lock at the garden gate, this one took her a lot longer to pick. Finally, it gave with a snick. She shoved the pins back into her wrap and cast a glance back at the dead spider fairy.

Cinder grabbed a lamp, then eased the door open and peered down the empty corridor, which gave way to blackness. She had come from the left before, so now she slipped into the corridor and turned right. Holding the light to the side, she strained to listen as she rushed down the hall. When she came to a place where one tunnel branched into three, she had counted 878 steps.

Smoke curled along the ceiling of one tunnel, which led up. In the second, Cinder could see pickaxes and buckets. The other tunnel, branching off to the right, smelled like human waste. Taking one of the pickaxes, she hustled down the tunnel to the right. She had to duck to not hurt her head, while making her way through rubble and debris.

In front of her, a light began to grow. Cinder blew out her lamp, slowed her steps, and crept forward, pickax raised just in case. What she saw stopped her cold. A man sat at a rickety table with a lantern, a game of white and black stones spread out in front of him. He wore a sword at his waist and was smoking something that smelled sweet. Just before him was an open pit with a rope ladder coiled at the side. They must be keeping the slaves here.

Staying in the shadows, Cinder shifted her grip on the pickax and slipped her other hand into her robe to pinch the snake. "If you're still alive, now would be the time to slither out and bite him," she whispered. The tongue flicked out, touching her fingers. The snake was alive, but barely able to move. "If I die, tell Darsam what happened to me," Cinder said softly.

She slid forward one step at a time until she was just out of range of the light. The man sat with his back against the wall—he'd see her if she took one more step. Steeling herself, she sprinted into the light, pickax raised. The man gave a startled shout and grasped his sword. He had it halfway out of his sheath when Cinder let the pickax fall forward. The point impaled the man where shoulder met neck. Blood sprayed Cinder, staining her in a way that she would never be able to wash away. He gasped and struggled to pull his sword free. But his knees buckled, his blood gushing down and spreading toward Cinder's feet. She let go of the pickax and jumped back before it could touch her. She turned her back on what she had done—what she'd had to do.

Hadn't she had to do it?

She dropped to her knees and called down the dank hole. "Ash? Storm?"

"Cinder?" her mother's voice called back.

Weak with relief, she dropped the end of the rope ladder into the pit. She watched it snap and undulate, hissing as it fell one rung at a time. Watched as filthy, ragged hands appeared, pulling up equally ragged people—one of them an old man. He paused to catch his breath.

"Who are you?" she asked, wondering if she needed the pickax.

His haunted eyes met hers. "We dig the tunnels. How do we get out?"

Why did Jatar need tunnels? Cinder swallowed her horror and pointed the way she'd come. "Follow the incense. It will lead you out." She hoped.

People appeared in a steady stream, but her mother and grandmother did not. "What's taking you so long?" she called down.

"Some of these people need help," chided her mother from below.

Cinder closed her eyes, trying to ignore the smell of the old man's blood mixing with rock as it ran in a diminishing stream into the pit. But the more she tried to ignore it, the louder it seemed to become. *Drip, drip, drip.*

Her mother and grandmother were the last to appear, as they were helping an old man climb out of the hole. Ash saw the dead guard, and her gaze flashed with horror and sympathy. Storm simply grasped Cinder's upper arms and shook her as if to dislodge the horror. "In war, to live is to kill. To protect is to kill. Remember that."

Cinder nodded and then followed her grandmother out the last few steps. They stole the man's lantern and ran steadily upward through the corridor. Cinder followed the smoke, only taking enough time to snatch another pickax from the ground. Finally, the low-ceilinged tunnel came to a dead end, with a hole above it. She jumped to catch the edge. Careful not to impale herself on the pickax, she pulled herself into what appeared to be an empty bedroom, a loose tile sitting off to the side.

She set the pickax aside and turned to help her mother and grandmother up. They carefully slid the tile back into place and peeked out the open doors. Dozens of doors stood open to what appeared to be empty rooms. From somewhere far away, Cinder could hear the sounds of fighting.

"Where are we?" Ash asked.

"I don't know." Adjusting her grip on the pickax, Cinder eased into the hallway, where light came in from high windows. She crept forward, straining to identify the objects in shadow. At the end of the hallway, a large golden pivot door stood slightly ajar. On the other side, a fountain trickled gently into a geometric pool. Cinder's mouth fell open as her gaze landed on the object in the water: a glass idol of the Goddess of Fire.

"We're in the temple," Ash whispered.

"That's right next to the lord's palace," Cinder said. She suddenly understood why Jatar had needed all those slaves; he'd been digging his way toward the palace. What better way to move his insurgents undetected?

"Where are all the priestesses?" Ash .

Cinder had no idea where Darsam was or why he hadn't come for her, and she had no time to find out. "Come on. We have to escape before Jatar returns."

They crossed the bethel and hurried into a courtyard of pools of water and trees, all of it surrounded by a short wall, not designed for defending against an army so much as keeping the populace out. They hadn't even descended all the steps when a dozen men rushed into the courtyard and slammed the gate behind them, sliding the bar over it just as something crashed into it from the other side. The group whirled toward them.

"Back inside," Ash hissed.

"You!" a familiar voice shouted. "You led us into a trap!"

It was Jatar, and he had spotted Cinder. Not daring to let go of the pickax for even a moment, she put her back into the heavy pivot door while her mother and grandmother pushed with all their might. They dropped the bar into place. She glanced around, relieved to find the dozens of other pivot doors between the columns shut and bolted tight. But her relief was short lived as an axe slammed into the door.

"What do we do?" Ash cried.

"The tunnels," Cinder said. "I think I can find my way back to the abandoned building." If they could just keep ahead of Jatar and his men, they could disappear into the city.

They ran back into what must have been the priestesses' bedrooms in the center of the temple, but in the dark, each one looked exactly like the others. The three women spread out, searching for the one with the loose tile. In the fifth room Cinder tried, the tile beneath her heel sounded hollow. She set down the pickax, then knelt, dug her fingers under the tile, and lifted it to reveal darkness below. "Here!" she cried, turning.

A hand buried itself in her hair, wrenching her off her feet and throwing her into the opposite wall. Her side throbbing and her scalp on fire, she looked up as a dozen shadowy figures slipped into the darkened room. She darted forward and grabbed the pickax before rounding on them.

"Back into the tunnels," Jatar growled to the other men. "Make for the warehouse. We'll slip out of the city as planned." The men dropped down into the darkness. From below, light appeared—someone must have lit a lamp or a torch. For the first time, Cinder could see the blood and gore that coated her captors, as well as herself. More men came into the room, two holding Ash and Storm.

"Let them go," Cinder growled, her pickax cocked back.

Lunging, Jatar brought the back of his sword down on her wrist. Her hand went numb, and the ax clattered from her grasp. He took hold of her hands, shoved them into a loop of rope, and pulled it tight. He pushed her into Durux's arms.

"You want us to kill the women?" A man asked.

"No," Jatar answered. "We'll take these three with us as hostages in case we run into any more trouble." Cinder shot her mother and grandmother a look of desperation as the slavers pushed them down the hole. The last man dropped in after them, leaving Cinder alone with Jatar and Durux.

"I would have preferred Naiba, but you will have to do," Durux said, his large ears pressed against her cheek.

Cinder cringed but then froze at the sound of shouts rising from the tunnels. A moment later came the sound of swords clanging discordantly.

"Tribesmen!" someone shouted from below. "At least a dozen of them."

"Darsam!" Cinder cried, hoping against hope it was him.

"Cinder!" he yelled back.

She kicked her heel against Durux, trying to break free. "My mother and grandmother are down there! Don't let them hurt—"

Durux's hand clamped down over her mouth as he pinned her to his chest. To his father, he whispered, "Our men are outnumbered two to one—we don't stand a chance."

"Hold them off!" Jatar called to those below. "We'll find another way out and come back for you!" He pushed his son back into the corridor. "We go over the back wall and disappear into the city."

"And the men?" Durux asked.

"We can always get more."

Cinder kicked and screamed and fought until Durux punched her in the temple. Her body went limp and he flipped her over his shoulder and ran to the back of the temple, into the priestesses' private bethel. Lamps burned in the circular channels of oil that surrounded golden pillars.

Ears ringing, Cinder pinched her eyes shut and tried to clear her head. If Jatar got her outside, she would never see her family or Darsam again. But Jatar had made her drop the pickax. Cinder had no other weapons.

Then she remembered the snake. But with her hands tied, she couldn't reach into her robes. She felt the skin of her wrists tear as she twisted them so they lay crosswise. She reached inside her robes and felt the flickering tongue against her fingers. Hoping the fairy would understand what she needed, Cinder pulled the snake from her robes. Her hands were tied and she was bouncing on Durux's shoulder. She fumbled the snake, nearly dropping Siseth. But she finally managed to get her fingers in the snake's mouth and pried it open. The fangs extended, venom dripping. She drove the snake into Durux's back.

He reared back with a shout, dropping Cinder hard on her backside. He reached behind him, ripped off the snake, and flung it at one of the pillars. Scrambling, Cinder ran back toward the tunnel entrance. There was a rushing sound, and then something solid connected with the back of her head. She collapsed, hitting her face hard. She struggled to push herself up, but her body wasn't responding. Blood spilled from her nose—she'd broken it. More blood ran through her hair and trickled around her earlobes before dripping off her chin. Distantly she wondered what Durux had thrown at the back of her head. She managed to roll onto her side, but she couldn't quite get her legs under her.

"A cobra!" Durux gasped. "I'm a dead man."

Jatar eyed his son. "Get to the healer before the poison sets in. Go!"

"What about you?"

Jatar's deadly stare fixed on Cinder. "I'll be right behind you."

Durux shot her a look of profound regret and took off running. She tried to push herself up, but her hands slipped in her own blood and she fell back. On her second attempt, she lugged herself away from Jatar, dragging her impossibly heavy limbs.

She heard his sword come free from its sheath as he stalked toward her. He grabbed her shoulder and flipped her onto her back, then stood over her, blade in hand. "You've cost me my insurrection. You've probably cost me my son's life. And—"

Jatar grunted as a knife grazed his shoulder. He glanced at something behind Cinder, then drove his blade toward her. Another sword caught it and threw it back. Darsam leapt over her, forcing Jatar back. The clanging and screeching of metal made Cinder's teeth hurt.

She staggered to her feet. Searching for a way to help Darsam, she caught sight of the snake. She made her way toward the creature, which was obviously badly injured but still alive. "Tell the goddess about the secret entrance to the tunnel," Cinder said to the snake. "Tell her that Darsam needs her help." Then Cinder crushed the snake's head beneath her boot, freeing the fairy to find another host body.

She turned back to the fight. Jatar was retreating from Darsam's furious onslaught. Darsam thrust, Jatar ducked and parried. Darsam took advantage and slid forward, but his foot slipped in Cinder's blood and he stumbled, his leg giving out beneath him. Jatar struck once, twice, three times.

Darsam managed to block. Barely. Cinder careened toward Jatar, who kicked Darsam's sword away. She barreled into the slaver, both of them crashing in a tangled heap. Cinder wrenched his knife from its scabbard and drove it toward him. It skittered off his ribs, cutting him badly, but not a killing wound. Dizzy and lightheaded, she scrambled back while Jatar struggled to stand. Darsam lunged to his feet to meet him, his sword arcing out. Jatar tried to block the blow but moved too slowly. Darsam recovered, his sword flashing and then slashing into Jatar's middle. Stunned, the man gaped at Darsam. Then Jatar's gaze slid to Cinder. She forced herself to meet his eyes, her chin up. His legs buckled and he landed face first on the tile floor. Darsam's sword moved swiftly down toward the slaver's neck.

Cinder looked away, but she heard the blade cut through flesh and bone to shatter the tile beneath. She stared at the body—no longer a man. Never again a threat. Just a pile of flesh and bones that would molder away. She let out a sob of relief.

"Are you all right?" Darsam asked as he cut her hands free.

Still dizzy, Cinder gave a little nod as she rubbed her bloody wrists. "I'll live."

"Stay here. I have to go back for my men."

But no sooner had he turned around than tribesmen appeared in the bethel, Ash behind their protective formation. "Cinder!" she cried and rushed across the room to throw her arms around her daughter. Storm was a step behind. Cinder held them tight, unable to shake the worry that someone would rip them out of her embrace if she let go for even a moment.

"Come on," Darsam said. "We have to get the three of you behind the palace walls." He ordered two of his tribesmen to take up the rear. The rest of the men hurried through the temple to the public bethel. Just as they stepped inside, twelve slavers carrying lanterns rushed in, some fearful, others furious.

Lanterns were set aside, and the two groups clashed in a wave of swinging swords. One of the tribesmen fell—Ashar. He scrambled back, crawling away from the line of battle and slipping in his own blood. Ash dove forward to grab his arm and pull him back to safety. Then she bent over him and pressed against his wounds to staunch the bleeding.

Sweat running down his body, Darsam battled against two men. Cinder took a step toward him, to help him somehow, but her grandmother pulled her back. "You'll only be in the way, child."

A flash of heat tore through the building. As one, the slavers tipped their heads back to scream, but they froze in a rictus of horror as their bodies turned red and then black and then gray. Then they collapsed into piles of ash.

On wings of white fire, Nelay flew into the room, a snake on her shoulder. She was dressed from head to toe in golden armor. She looked around at the dead men and raised her face to Darsam. "All the cities of Idara are under attack. Keep Arcina under your control. Keep my son safe. I fly to Thanjavar, to protect the rest of my family."

She pumped her massive wings, the downstroke sending a blast of heat that singed Cinder's eyebrows and made the lamps flicker. And then the goddess queen was gone.

"We have to reach the palace, Sam," Ashar spoke up from where he lay under Ash's care. She had bandaged his leg and managed to stop the bleeding.

Darsam's gaze swept the group. Three were too injured to walk. "We can't risk enough men to carry them. We'll have to make a stand here and hope we're not overwhelmed."

"We can carry them," Cinder said.

His face half in shadow from the lamplight, Darsam assessed her. He gave a curt nod. "Back into formation."

Ash, Storm, and Cinder each took an injured man on their backs and fell into line. With lamps held aloft at the front and rear of the group, they moved as fast as they dared through the darkened streets. Thankfully, no one assaulted them, and steps later they reached the palace gates unscathed. Palace guards took Cinder's burden from her arms.

Darsam hurried over to her. "The palace has remained secure, but I have to go continue through the city—to put an end to this threat so it can never rise up again."

Cinder shivered as the wind blew across the blood drying on her clothes. "Durux is still out there, though he was bit by a cobra."

Darsam's mouth tightened. "Get inside. You'll be safe." He started to turn away.

"Yula—Naiba . . . Is she safe?"

"Already on her way home." He whirled back and pressed his mouth to Cinder's in a hard kiss. Calling for his men, he slipped out the gate without a backward glance.

CHAPTER FIFTEEN

Cinder woke in the middle of the night to the rumbling of thunder and the incessant flash of lightning. Moving carefully so as not to hurt her head, she looked over at her slumbering mother and grandmother. Outside, the rain started coming down again. Cinder tried to go back to sleep, but the events of the last few weeks kept playing in her head.

Finally, she gave up. Careful not to wake her family, she pushed herself out of the silken covers. She opened a chest at the foot of the bed, cringing as it groaned, but her family didn't stir. She took out a simple but finely made robe and wrapped it around herself, then tied it off. She stepped onto the balcony to retrieve her sandals as lightning skipped across the base of the clouds.

"He drew my attention."

Cinder started and followed the voice to find what had to be a fairy crouching on the railing. Lightning flickered, revealing her features—almond-shaped eyes, flat face, slitted nose. Thick coils of hair gathered atop her head. Her scaly wings were folded at her back and matched the scales that covered most of her torso.

Cinder gasped. "Siseth?"

The fairy cocked her head to the side. "So I killed him."

Cinder was struggling to understand, to get her sleepy mind to put everything together, when something dropped down in front of her and dangled before her face. Another fairy, upside down. In addition to the eyes on its face, six bulbous eyes protruded from a mane of coarse, spiky hair. Her wings were woven of spider silk, and she wore what looked like a fur collar and a short, thick fur skirt. "We were angry. We wanted to hurt him. So we did. For a long time. We are not angry anymore."

"Durux," Cinder said.

Both fairies grinned, revealing glistening fangs. "It is an honor that we allow you to see us, mortal woman," Siseth said.

Cinder found it hard to keep calm in their otherworldly, feral presence. "What have I done to deserve such an honor?"

"You saved our queen," Siseth said.

With that, both fairies blurred and were gone. Disturbed, Cinder walked as calmly as she could back into her room and locked the balcony doors. Not that she thought that would keep any fairies out, but it made her feel better.

She leaned against the doors, her eyes slipping closed in relief. He was dead. Durux was dead, and he would never be able to hurt anyone again.

Knowing she wouldn't be able to sleep for a long while, Cinder left the room and walked the palace halls. Even at this late hour, servants were about, rushing down the halls with bandages, bowls of water, and food to tend to the wounded. Used to the sight of Cinder, who had been in the palace for nearly two weeks, they paid her no mind as she wandered into Darsam's dark room. She closed her eyes as the smell of him enveloped her. She'd come here many times over the last few weeks—it was one of the only places she felt truly safe.

She shut the door soundlessly, and her practiced feet slipped across the stone floor. She stood at the window, looking down into the bailey in hopes he would be there. He was working to uproot any insurrectionist who still remained, and Cinder tried not to worry about him. Just then she realized she had walked the halls for at least an hour and hadn't counted any of her steps. Since meeting Darsam, she'd been counting less and less, maybe because she didn't need the numbers as much anymore.

Lightning flashed again, burning into her retinas. Shivering, she eased into Darsam's bed and wrapped herself up in his blankets.

She nearly screamed when an arm wrapped around her.

"Cinder, do you often slip into men's beds in the middle of the night?"

"Darsam?" she squealed. She rolled over and took his face in her hands, her fingers skimming over him to make sure he was really all right. When she got to his chest and found he wasn't wearing a shirt, her search stumbled to a halt and she breathed in a silent gasp.

"I'm fine."

Cinder threw her arms around him. "I've been so worried about you."

"I can tell." He winced a little, so she released him.

"You *are* hurt," she accused.

"Just bruised and cut up a bit." He chuckled softly. "I thought my bed smelled a little like you. I decided it must just be wishful thinking."

She bit her lip, suddenly aware that she was in Darsam's bed. It wasn't the first time she had been beside him like this, but that was before. "Are you back for good now?"

"For a little while. But Nelay's spies keep finding more rebels that need put down. It may take a few weeks more before we've rooted them all out." Darsam was silent for a time. "Cinder, I'm so sorry, but we haven't found Durux yet."

"He's dead."

"How can you be sure?"

"The fairies told me."

Darsam sucked in a breath. "It's a dangerous thing to anger a fairy. But I can't say he didn't have it coming to him."

Cinder tucked her forehead into Darsam's chest, grateful to him in ways she could never repay. "When did you get back?" she asked.

"A few hours ago."

"And I woke you."

"I don't mind."

She hesitated. "Darsam, when I left the palace that night, the guards called me 'one of Darsam's girls', like you have girls with you all the time."

He nuzzled against her. "It's easier than explaining that they're my spies."

Cinder relaxed against him, reveling in the feeling of his arms around her. He stroked her head, pausing when he felt the growth on the sides of her scalp. "You're letting it grow in?"

"They changed my tattoo to that of a slave. I'm still not sure who owns me now."

"No one owns you, Cinder. No one ever did."

She closed her eyes, feeling herself opening up to this selfless, beautiful man. "My grandmother wants to go back to the clanlands." Darsam didn't reply, and Cinder wished it was light so she could read his expression. "My mother isn't so keen," she continued. "She's been visiting Ashar every day. And she's started to smile with her whole body whenever she's around him."

"Ash and Ashar. You couldn't have planned that."

Cinder paused. "I don't . . .I don't know what to do."

"You don't have to decide anything tonight," Darsam told her. "You're alive. I'm alive. For now, that is enough."

175

Cinder awoke to the door creaking open and a startled gasp. Her eyes shot open to find her mother and grandmother at the threshold. It wasn't the first time they had found Cinder curled up in Darsam's bed. She became aware of the weight of his arm around her. He pushed himself up on the crook of his arm, and Cinder blushed as she remembered he wasn't wearing a shirt.

"He was here when I came in last night," Cinder blurted. "I was so happy he was all right that we talked for half the night. I fell asleep."

"How dare you take advantage of her!" Storm said.

Ash laid a hand on her mother's arm and said, "You've been summoned by the goddess."

Darsam flipped off the covers and got out of bed. "She's in the city? Did she say why?"

"Not you," Ash corrected. "She wants to see Cinder."

Darsam froze for a moment before he moved to grab a medium-sized chest at the end of the bed. "Here, I retrieved these for you." He placed the trunk at the foot of the bed and then moved to kiss Cinder's forehead. "Clean yourself up, eat something. I'll see you there." She took a shaky breath and nodded. "It's going to be fine, Cinder. You saved her life and the life of her family. There's no reason to be afraid."

She nodded again, took the trunk, and turned to follow her mother, as her grandmother had already stormed down the hall. Back in their shared room, her grandmother was pacing. The moment they stepped in, she started gesturing wildly. "He's an Idaran, Cinder! He's no different than the men who have killed, enslaved, and raped our people for the last three generations!"

"He risked his life to save us," Cinder reminded her grandmother as she set the chest on a small table.

Storm snorted. "Risked his life? He's the lord's son. He was never in any danger from the city watchmen."

"What of the risk he took with Jatar?" Ash said quietly.

Storm turned angry eyes to her daughter. "You're no better. You spend all your time with that tribesman. Aren't you sick of men possessing you?"

Ash blanched. "Evil resides in the hearts of men *and* women. Ashar is one of the kindest people I've ever met."

Storm worked her jaw. "We're free—all of us. We're going back to the clanlands to be with my family. That's the end of it." She left, slamming the door behind her so hard Cinder jumped.

Cinder opened the chest, which held the dresses she'd made so long ago. As she let her hand trail across the golden silk, her eyes filled with tears to think she hadn't told Darsam she had wanted to be a seamstress with her whole heart. That she'd spent hours making her dresses. And yet he'd known. Gone to Zura's to fetch them for her.

"I have no memory of the clanlands," Ash said.

Neither did Cinder. "She's right, though. They are our people."

Ash gestured to the small table, which Cinder now noticed held a bowl of fruit and bread. "Hurry and eat, Cinder. It's probably a bad idea to keep a goddess queen waiting."

Wearing a green dress of her own design, Cinder stepped into the throne room with her mother and grandmother at her sides. Nelay sat on her throne with her son, Denar, next to her. Cinder let out a silent sigh of relief to see the young man looking healthy. He even winked at her. She tried to smile, but her mouth didn't seem to be working properly. She wiped her sweaty palms on her dress and eased into the room, scanning faces for any clue as to why the goddess had summoned her. The majority of people present were guild leaders; the rest were soldiers, many of whom were injured.

At the front of the group, just to the right of the dais, stood Darsam with a handful of children who so resembled him they had to be his siblings. Behind Nelay were Bahar and Maran. Next to the queen stood a man whose tattoos named him as Bahar's heir, which meant he was Darsam's oldest brother and future lord of Arcina.

Darsam gave Cinder a reassuring smile. Reminding herself that she had saved them all, she lifted her chin and walked straight toward the throne, her gaze straying neither to the left or right. When she finally stopped, she became aware of an ache in her chest, a burning tightness. But she made no outward sign.

The goddess rose to her feet. "Cinder, daughter of Ash, who is daughter of Storm, it is because of you that we were prepared for this insurrection. That we survived it. You saved my life, and my son's life. My husband tells me I must offer you a boon. So I shall. Name anything you want up to a lordship over one of my cities, and it shall be yours."

Cinder blinked in shock. She turned slowly to face her mother and grandmother. She had everything she wanted. They were free. She was free. But then Cinder thought back to the other companions—and the women who would replace them.

She turned back to the goddess. "I want slavery abolished and brothels outlawed."

Beside the dais, Darsam broke into a proud grin.

Nelay considered Cinder. "To what end? No one will hire those of clannish descent. No one wants them here."

"Then let them go back to the clanlands, if they wish," Cinder said. "Back to their homes and families."

The queen considered her. "Those like you, who are half clannish and half Idaran, have not been well received by the clannish."

It hadn't occurred to Cinder that she could be hated for her Idaran blood just as much in the clanlands as she was for her clannish blood in Idara. "I—I don't know, Goddess," she stuttered.

Nelay sat back in her throne, fingers trapping. "So you would orchestrate their freedom and then abandon them?"

Cinder's jaw worked.

"How is that her responsibility?" Storm asked suddenly.

Nelay's burning stare fell on Cinder's grandmother. "We have been fighting to pass this law for two decades." For once, Storm fell silent. The goddess's gaze went back to Cinder and softened a little. "If I pass this law, there will be repercussions. Are you willing to deal with them?"

This would mean she could not return to the clanlands. Cinder glanced at Darsam, and in that moment she realized she did not want to leave him. Not yet, anyway. She turned at her grandmother.

The older woman looked crestfallen, even devastated. "She's right, Cinder. The clans hate Idarans. Many of the half-breeds" —Storm winced at the word— "might not even be welcome. And to be honest, maybe I don't want to go back to the people who abandoned me after I gave my life to save them."

Is that what Cinder would be to the clanspeople? A half-breed? When she dropped her head and caught sight of her dress, an idea came to her. "Let them work for me. Making my designs."

"Who would wear the designs of a one-time slave?" a woman hissed from the crowd. "I for one—" She cut off abruptly as her hair started to smoke.

Cinder decided she almost liked this queen. "If the goddess wears them, and her priestesses, will not Idara love them?" she said.

A slow smile spread across the queen's face. "I believe they will." She raised an eyebrow. "So, you will see your people are taken care of?"

Cinder nodded. "I will."

The queen eyed her shrewdly. "Then you may start by deciding what is to be done with the slave owners." At the wave of her hand, several guards came into the room. Between them were Zura, Magian, Farush, and Farood. Cinder's breath caught. She'd never wanted to see this woman or her daughters or her lackeys again.

"I have been told," Nelay went on, "that there are hundreds, perhaps thousands, of men and women who own slaves throughout Idara. What would you do with them?"

Cinder let out a long exhale and turned to Darsam. "Were they part of the uprising?"

He shook his head. "Not that we can find."

"Kill them." Ash's voice shook with fury. "Take them down to that horrible cellar and beat every inch of them. Then let them starve."

Zura stomped her foot. "I treated my slaves far better than most masters. I was firm yet fair."

"You manipulated and used us," Ash growled, "to make yourself wealthy and important. You know you used us and that what you did was wrong."

"But not illegal," Zura said through clenched teeth.

"Just because it was legal, doesn't mean it was moral," Ash responded.

"Shall I kill them?" Nelay asked, flames dancing across her fingers. "Reduce them to ash?"

Zura's mouth came open. "My queen, my goddess! Surely you don't mean to kill every slave owner in all of Idara."

"I've killed many people for less."

Zura licked her lips and slowly lowered to her knees. Magian was a beat behind her. Then Farush and Farood. "I beg you, Goddess," Zura said.

Nelay shrugged. "Don't beg me. I'm not the one who will decide." She nodded toward Cinder. "She will."

Zura's face went pale and she turned to Cinder. "Please."

Cinder's gaze went back to the queen. She knew the older woman was testing her to see what she would do. And she knew if she killed her former master and her lackeys, slave owners throughout Idara would rise up to defend themselves. More lives would be lost. More slaves killed.

"I won't kill you," Cinder said.

Relief washed across Zura's face.

"No!" Ash cried. "You can't. After all she's done to our family!"

"Hatred begets hatred, Mother. If this is ever to end, someone has to offer forgiveness." Cinder turned back to her former mistress and held up a finger. "I won't kill you . . . if you donate your fortune and the House of Night to right the wrongs you have done."

Zura clutched her throat. "What?"

"The freed slaves will need somewhere to go," Cinder said. "Somewhere large with plenty of bedrooms. And money to invest in cloth."

Zura sagged on her heels. "All of it?"

"Save the clothes on your backs," Cinder replied in a flash of anger.

Zura looked like she might throw up, but then she glanced at the queen and nodded. "Of course. I would be happy to donate to the cause."

Nelay waved to a handful of guards. "Go and secure the house. Make sure no one goes in or out until Cinder arrives to take an accounting."

Zura rose shakily to her feet and turned to go.

"Are you forgetting something?" Cinder asked coldly. Zura turned to look at her with a blank look on her face. "I said you could keep your clothes. Not your jewelry."

Zura hesitated before taking off her jewels and setting them on the floor. Magian followed suit.

"Now you may go." Cinder said.

The woman and her entourage left without another word. Cinder watched them go, surprised to feel her anger disappear. She hoped she would never have to see Zura again, or her thugs.

Nelay turned to Bahar and Maran. "See that Cinder has whatever she needs." The goddess rose to her feet. "Well, Denar, I think your visit with your cousins is over."

He leaned forward, resting his elbows on his knees, his gaze fixed on Cinder. "I'd like to stay."

Nelay rolled her eyes. "She's too old for you." She leaned closer to her son. "And I think she's spoken for."

Denar shot Darsam a look of mock disgust. "You have all the fun in Arcina."

Darsam grinned at his cousin.

Nelay stood from the throne and walked down the aisle, tendrils of fire uncurling from her back. "Come along, Son. Our chariot is waiting."

Denar trailed reluctantly behind her. "You're not just flying home?" he asked hopefully.

The queen chuckled. "Someone has to make sure you aren't sidetracked into another adventure."

"Haven't I earned my own name?" Denar asked.

Nelay gave him a reproachful glance. "You will carry the name of my father until you earn your second name. Such is the way of the tribesmen, your father's people."

"I saved the girl," Denar protested.

"I hardly think sneaking off after your cousin's rescue party and nearly getting yourself killed earns you anything," Nelay said.

With a dramatic sigh, Denar paused before Cinder, then took her hand and kissed it with a flourish. "Farewell, lovely lady! If ever again you should find yourself in need of rescuing, skip the bumbling mess that is my cousin and come straight to my competent arms." Despite herself, Cinder found a smile turning the corners of her mouth.

Denar shot a triumphant look at Darsam. "Make sure she keeps that smile on. It was a lot of working coaxing it out." Whistling, Denar headed off after his mother.

Cinder turned to watch him go. "That boy is going to be trouble," she murmured to Darsam as he came to her side.

"He already is." There was laughter in Darsam's voice. "But it's never a dull moment when he's around." Darsam turned to Cinder with a determined expression. "I will assist you."

She blinked at him. "How?"

"Same way I've always done—helping those who need it." When she didn't answer, his gaze dropped uncertainly. "That is, if you want my help."

Storm rolled her eyes. "Is there any way to get rid of him?"

Cinder glared at her grandmother, who threw her hands in the air and hurried off.

Darsam stepped a little closer. "Well?"

Cinder reached out to take his hand. "I would be honored."

EPILOGUE

The next few months were a whirlwind of activity. All of the clannish and Luathan slaves did not receive their freedom at once. Rather, they were collected from their owners and taken to a makeshift city of tents, where they could take one of three options: work for Cinder, work in the Luminash mines, or secure passage back to their homelands. Most took the passage. But many of the half-breeds stayed on—younger people who, like Cinder, could not remember their ties to their homes.

Darsam was always by her side, helping her, counseling her, protecting her. Slowly, Storm began to soften towards him. Ash began spending more and more time with Ashar, who was quiet and kind and one of the smartest people Cinder had ever met.

Within a year, all the slaves were free, and Cinder had a thriving business in Idara. One day as she sat in one of her shops, working on her accounts, she looked up to see her grandmother walk through the doorway. "I have said yes," Storm declared.

Cinder blinked at her. "What?"

Her grandmother only patted her granddaughter's head and said, "But that doesn't mean you have to."

She left the room as abruptly as she'd come. Cinder stared after her in bewilderment as Darsam came inside and leaned against one of the tent poles. She went back to struggling over the numbers. "Do you know what this is all about?" she asked him.

"Remember when your grandmother said I was an Idaran and couldn't be trusted?"

Cinder nodded.

"Well, I pestered her enough that she finally made me a deal. If I proved myself loyal for a year, I could marry you." Cinder felt her cheeks turn hot. "She's a little untrusting of men—understandably," Darsam continued. "And Idarans."

Cinder pressed her hands to her cheeks. "Marry you?"

He came to kneel beside her desk. "You have the choice. Go back to clanlands. Or stay. With me." She stared at him openmouthed. "We can make our home in the Adrack," he said. "You would love it. And my family there . . . they would love you." He took her hands in his. "Cinder, Nelay listens to you. Idara needs you to be a part of things. I need you."

"Darsam, I don't think I could deny you anything." She leaned forward, and two lips, two bodies, two hearts melded into one.

Loved this?
Then continue with the next book in the
Fairy Queens Series by purchasing
Daughter of Winter
(http://amberargyle.com/daughterofwinter/)

AUTHOR'S NOTE

O*f Sand and Storm* is a dark story—it deals with slavery and sex trafficking. A part of me wants to apologize for this—for exposing such darkness to the light. But even today, there are people hidden in those shadows. If no one ever turns to look, help will never come. So I ask that you look. See them—those forced to give up the right to their own bodies. I ask that you be someone's Darsam.

To learn how you can help, visit the Abolitionists, a group who works to free children from sex trafficking:

http://ourrescue.org/

ACKNOWLEDGMENTS

Thanks go out to my amazing editing team: Charity West (content editor), Linda Prince (copy editor), and Cathy Nielson (proofreader), Rachel Newswander (proofreader); and my talented design team: Lara Sava (illustrator), Michelle Argyle (graphic designer), Julie Titus (formatter), and Bob Defendi (map maker).

My everlasting love to Derek, Corbin, Lily, Connor, and God.

Amber Argyle is the bestselling author of the Witch Song series and the Fairy Queen series. Her books have been nominated for and won awards and have been translated into French and Indonesian.

Amber graduated cum laude from Utah State University with a degree in English and physical education, a husband, and a two-year-old. Since then, she and her husband have added two more children, which they are actively trying to transform from crazy small people into less crazy larger people.

Visit Amber Argyle's website to sign up for her free starter library or to learn more: amberargyle.com

OTHER TITLES BY AMBER ARGYLE

Witch Song Series

Witch Song
Witch Born
Witch Rising
Witch Fall

Fairy Queens Series

Of Ice and Snow
Winter Queen
Of Fire and Ash
Summer Queen
Of Sand and Storm
Daughter of Winter
Winter's Heir